CW01024333

Mediterranean Ghost Stories

by

Ozzie Kent

For Paul

CONTENTS

THE WOLVES OF RAVENNA

Ravenna is one of the most interesting and beautiful cities in Italy, known for the colourful mosaics adorning many of its churches and basilicas. I was on the last day of a short stay in the city, and had already visited most of the sites. I had started the morning, as all my other mornings, by heading for a coffee and croissant in the nearby Piazza del Popolo, which today was thronging with people, as it was market day. I passed stalls selling jams and chutneys, cheeses and hams, fruits and vegetables, and the ubiquitous touristy trinkets and jewellery.

I stopped in front of one dedicated to selling Venetian masks, even though Venice was over a hundred kilometres away. The stallholder had arranged all the masks, many with colourful feathers attached, facing out to the viewer. I could almost imagine eyes behind the masks looking down at me through the slots; a little unnerving. The stallholder greeted me with a 'Buongiorno', and asked if he could assist me in the purchase of one. I wished him good morning in return and told him how beautiful they all were, but politely declined.

I chose a different café that day, at a corner of the square near to the clock tower, and found a table facing out so that I could enjoy a bit of people-watching. No sooner had I sat down than a waiter appeared and handed a menu to me. I already knew what I wanted, and so ordered in my best Italian without opening the menu, instead handing it back to the waiter, who promptly disappeared into the café.

The morning felt chilly, even though the sun was shining directly on the café; but I was suitably wrapped up to sit outside, considering it was still early January. Next to me was an outdoor gas heater, which all the cafés and restaurants around the square seemed to have. Soon the waiter arrived with my order.

I ate the croissant and sipped the coffee, watching all the shoppers. Several had bicycles with baskets at the front into which they placed their purchases; others simply carried them in plastic bags provided by the vendors. It was encouraging to see them marked as bio-degradable. A couple with a young boy caught my attention, standing together in front of a man selling helium-filled balloons of various animals. I watched as the boy pointed out the one he wanted, but each time the man seemed to give him the wrong one. Eventually, he stamped his feet on the ground after being offered the wrong one for the third time. It was not really the vendor's fault, as a slight breeze was turning the balloons around and around; but on the fourth attempt the boy was pleased to be handed his chosen animal balloon at last, and his parents paid the vendor.

I finished my coffee and turned to the waiter, gesturing to him to bring me the bill, and then turned my attention back to watch the family as they approached the café. At first sight, the balloon looked like a dog with pointed ears, but all I could now see was the back of the balloon, as the wind had turned it away from me. I smiled at the family as they passed and they smiled back, perhaps realising that I must have been amused by their son's antics. Then the breeze turned the boy's balloon around once again, and I saw the front. I saw the face of a wolf, with large nasty looking teeth and huge staring eyes. The stare seemed so real that it transfixed me for a few seconds, only releasing me when the face gently turned around to the direction the family were heading. I gave a nervous laugh and found the waiter standing next to me with the bill in his hand.

He placed it on the table and gave me a strange look before attending to a nearby couple. I left a few euros on the table and looked back towards the family, but they had left the square.

I had decided that I would visit the National Museum that morning, the last item on my itinerary for my visit to Ravenna. I set off across the Piazza del Popolo, consulting Google maps on my phone. The museum was only a short walk from the piazza, and on arriving at the entrance, I was pleasantly surprised that no one was queuing at the ticket office. I guessed they were all shopping at the market, or engaged in other outdoor activities, as it was such a bright sunny morning.

Starting on the ground floor I strolled at a leisurely pace around the rooms housing the museum collections. I viewed artefacts made of ivory, Renaissance bronzes, icons, and a section dedicated to ceramics. Another room displayed a collection of ancient weapons which I glanced at briefly, then moved on to have a look at various decorated sarcophagi and marble column capitals, which were much more interesting. After an hour or so I ascended a marble staircase to the first floor, pushing open a nearby door to arrive at the start of a long vaulted corridor. On the left-hand side was a white painted wall, opposite which a series of windows ran the full length of the corridor. Bright sunlight cast strange shadows onto the wall as it filtered through a line of tall cypress trees outside in a courtyard garden.

Along the wall were displayed several marble statues placed evenly apart. As I walked, observing them, the shadows flickered against the wall and the statues. The whole corridor was empty of visitors except for me; not even a museum curator was in sight, just an empty black chair where one would normally sit at the entrance to the corridor. I stopped in front of a familiar bronze sculpture, the famous she-wolf of Rome, known as the Capitoline Wolf. It depicted a scene from the legend of the founding of Rome; a she-wolf suckling the mythical twins, Romulus and Remus.

There was an eerie silence as I bent down to look at the information plaque next to the sculpture. I had got as far as reading that it was a copy of the original, when something made me gasp and straighten up. I had seen the shadow of something momentarily moving across the wall, and instinctively turned round to the window behind me, but I saw nothing, only the trees outside. I hurried to the window and looked out both ways along the balcony outside as far as it was possible to see, but again - nothing.

My heart was racing, and I jumped when the door at the far end swung open. A museum curator appeared. He walked towards me, somewhat puzzled by my reaction to seeing him, and said 'Buongiorno' as he passed. He went and sat on the black chair at the entrance, then looked at back me and smiled before pulling out a phone from his pocket. He began tapping at the keys. I smiled back at him nervously, although he was no longer looking at me.

I made my way to the opposite end of the corridor, glancing quickly at the last two sculptures along the wall, before pushing open the door that the curator had just come through. I found myself in a vaulted square room with a floor of red brick tiles. Directly opposite I could see a swing door leading to another gallery. I looked at the wall to my right to see if there was another door leading to the balcony outside, but there wasn't. So the access onto the balcony must be from a door at the entrance to the corridor behind me, I thought. I consulted the museum floor plan on a nearby panel and confirmed that this was the case. The information on the lower part of the panel gave an overview of the artwork in the room. Now much calmer, I started to look at the Renaissance paintings on the walls, spending a few minutes on each piece. Soon I was lost in the themes of the paintings, remarking to myself how splendid they were. I took my time, reading the information next to each painting, expanding my understanding of what the artist was trying to convey.

I was satisfied that I had done justice to the artwork in this room, and felt a little bit guilty that I had rushed through those on the ground floor. Consulting the floor plan again, I saw that there was one room left to visit, and so I made my way in that direction. Pushing open a heavy wooden swing door, I entered the room, letting the door gently swing shut on its own behind me.

Instantly I froze, for there in the centre of the room were three sculptured wolves, looking towards me. How bizarre, I thought. What on earth were they doing in a gallery exhibiting Renaissance painting? I spotted a panel beside the nearest sculpture and moved closer to read what it said. The sculptures were made by a modern artist, whose name I had never heard of before, and the material used was a type of grey clay. The panel explained how the surface of the wolves had been deliberately left rough, the clay having been freely applied and left without much smoothing, giving the impression of a muddy, matted coat. It certainly was effective in giving the wolves a realistic look. I walked around the first one and suddenly shuddered; the wolf felt alive, as if any minute it was going to pounce on me and sink its teeth into my neck. Its eyes seemed to follow me, searching for an opportunity.

I banished the thought from my head and returned to the paintings on the walls, moving back to study the first one by the swing door through which I had entered the room. I stared at it, but saw nothing, as I couldn't help thinking of the wolves behind me in the middle of the red brick tiled floor. Were they really watching me? Feeling uneasy, I moved sideways to view the next painting on the wall. As I did, I couldn't stop myself from glancing over my shoulder. I held my breath. Had the wolves moved? Was I being ridiculous? I turned around fully and looked at them. Surely they seemed to be in different positions... or was it simply because I was now viewing them from a different angle? Stop being paranoid, I thought to myself, and turned back to concentrate on the painting in front of me.

Moving to the next wall, I stood and scanned the four more Renaissance paintings exhibited, and made an effort to read all the information provided. I studied the paintings in detail, yet all the time I felt a creeping uneasiness, convinced I was being watched by the wolves. Unable to concentrate as much as I would have liked, I glanced back at them a few times to make sure they hadn't moved. What was I thinking? Of course they hadn't, they were just sculptures in a museum.

I made up my mind to touch the nearest sculpture to me, to reassure myself that it was, indeed, made of clay. I walked over and slowly reached out to one of its ears, running my hand over it several times and was pleased that it felt cold and like clay. Then – horror! - when I realised the ear had come off in my hand! What had I done?

I was startled when the swing door opened and a young couple entered the room. The girl gave a little scream, then laughed when she saw the wolf sculptures. I discreetly placed the clay ear I was holding into my pocket hoping neither of them had seen me.

The young man with the girl laughed too and started to tease her for being scared. He walked over and patted one, to show her there was nothing to be scared of. I felt ashamed of my earlier uneasiness. Fortunately they had still not noticed the missing ear. I felt guilty standing there with it in my pocket. The man put his arm around his girlfriend and they proceeded to walk around the room, briefly glancing at the paintings before heading to a side door. I followed, and the man politely held the door open for me. I took this as my cue to leave as well before a museum curator appeared and noticed the missing ear. I thanked him and stood by the door, waiting for the young couple to disappear so that I could return to the room and place the broken ear on the floor by the wolf.

As I glanced back into the room, a sudden chill ran up my spine and I stood there motionless. The wolf with the missing ear had turned its head to look at me; hackles raised, its eyes seeming to glow red. The hairs stood up on the back of my neck then the adrenaline kicked in. I let go of the door and almost ran to the exit down a stone staircase, passing the young couple on the way. They looked at me rather bemused, but I no longer cared what anyone thought. I dashed out of the museum into the bright sunshine, and only then stopped to catch my breath. Had I just witnessed the wolf sculpture coming to life? Or was it just a trick of the sunlight coming through the window? The more I thought of it the more I was able to persuade myself that it must have been the latter, but I wasn't really convinced. I knew what I had seen.

When I arrived back where I was staying, I took the clay ear out of my pocket and placed it on the table in the sitting room. What was I going to do with it? I knew I ought to return it to the museum, but if I did, they would accuse me of damaging the artwork. What would they do? A fine? Perhaps even prison? I eventually decided that I would carefully package it up and post it to the museum anonymously before I left the following morning.

That night I had trouble sleeping. I kept thinking about my visit to the museum and the wolf sculptures. Now they were really coming to life, prowling nearby, looking for me, trying to catch my scent... I must have eventually fallen asleep, but soon woke again. I looked to see what time it was - three in the morning.

I lay there willing myself to sleep, when all of a sudden I seemed to hear a distant howl break the stillness of the night. At first I assumed it was the local dogs, howling at the moon, but as the sound got nearer it changed to a deep growling noise.

I sensed movement outside the window of my ground floor bedroom. I pulled the duvet close around me, peering over the top. Through the thin curtains I could just make out a dark shadow, and – yes – a pair of red glowing eyes. Then came a scratching noise at the window, as if claws were being dragged across the glass, followed by a blood curdling growl that seem to go on forever. My heart thumped against my chest as I searched desperately for the light switch; finding it I snapped it on and flooded the room with light. The awful sound ceased.

I listened again, not daring to breathe. But all was silence, broken after a few moments by the hoot of an owl outside. I eventually lay down again, and must have fallen asleep at some point, but the night seemed long and I awoke tired and drained with the sunlight coming through the curtains and the electric light still on.

As I packed, I kept on glancing at the clay ear of the wolf on the table. I knew I would have no peace until I was rid of it. I wrapped it carefully in kitchen towel and placed it in a plastic bag. I would visit the Post Office on the way to the railway station; they would be sure to have a suitable padded envelope. The route took me past the National Museum. I had plenty of time before catching my train, so I decided to stop for a coffee at a cafe opposite the museum.

As I sat there, a large delivery van turned up and parked in front of the museum. The driver got out and walked into the side entrance. A few minutes later a museum curator came out clutching a board with some papers clipped to it. She was followed by the van driver, holding one of the wolf sculptures, heavily wrapped but still identifiable. He placed it in the back of the van shutting the door behind. It must have been the one with the missing ear, perhaps being sent back to the artist for repair. I had a terrible feeling of guilt, knowing here I was with the missing ear in my pocket.

The driver signed the papers the woman was holding, then, as she disappeared back into the museum, he got into his van and drove away from the museum. To my surprise he stopped right outside the cafe and got out, heading inside for a coffee. I turned to watch him as he chatted at the bar with the owner.

Then - I heard a low growling sound coming from the back of the van, and the door started to shake, as if something inside was trying to get out. This wasn't my imagination or a dream this time, it was as real as the coffee on the table before me; of that I had no doubt whatsoever. I put my hand in my pocket and took out the plastic bag containing the wolf's ear. The driver had left the van window low, and his attention was diverted. It was now or never. I stood up, leant forward, and threw the bag onto the passenger seat of the van. I was sitting down again sipping my coffee as the driver reappeared.

He got into the van and drove off, having noticed nothing. I could just hear a faint howl, fading to nothing as the van turned a street corner. At last I began to breathe a little easier, and, after paying for my coffee, I headed to the railway station, a spring in my step.

THE HARLEQUINS OF VIAREGGIO

The Carnival of Viareggio is an annual event that takes place in the Tuscan city of that name, and dates back to 1873, when the first such event took place. Back then, a group of the rich young bourgeoisie organised a parade of floats which were decorated with flowers, but some of the citizens of Viareggio decided to wear masks as a sign of protest against the high taxes that they were forced to pay. Since that time, the carnival has grown and grown, and now comprises numerous huge floats with caricatures of well known people, such as politicians, showmen and sports figures, as well as imaginary grotesque creatures, all built of papier-mâché.

Kevin Williams had made a special trip to Viareggio. He was a journalist employed by a major newspaper in London, and was delighted to have been chosen by the editor of the travel section to write an article about the carnival for the weekend travel supplement. Kevin knew that the reason was probably because his command of the Italian language was the best in the office, and teased his work colleagues in his usual cocky fashion, making them extremely envious.

Kevin arrived at his hotel by taxi from the nearby airport of Pisa, all paid for by the newspaper, of course. In fact, he could claim all his expenses for the next few days from his employer, and he was pleased the trip was not costing him a penny. He could even have a day or two as holiday, and claim that too. He looked up at the three storey building that was the hotel, and admired the flags and other decorations that were in the process of being put up by a man on a tall ladder, with another positioned on the pavement below, holding it for him. Several of the images displayed were of 'The Burlamacco', a clown-like, harlequin figure, which had been adopted as the town's mascot. A competition had been held in 1931 for the design, and had been won by Uberto Bonetti. He had chosen the red and white of the mascot's outfit after the traditional colours of the umbrellas on the beach at Viareggio. Kevin had done some research back in London, and had decided to include these historical facts in his article for the newspaper.

On entering the hotel, Kevin was amazed at the decoration of the lobby. All of the available wall space was taken up by framed posters of the Burlamacco mascot from previous years of the carnival. He was delighted when he approached the reception desk to see behind it a lady receptionist made up to look like Burlamacco.

'Buongiorno,' said the receptionist.

'Buongiorno!' replied Kevin, enthusiastically.

She asked him if he had a reservation, and asked for his passport. On realising he was from the UK, she spoke to him in English from then onwards.

Kevin was allocated a room on the top floor, with a balcony overlooking the "Passenggiata a Mare", the promenade along which all the floats are paraded. He opened the doors to the balcony and stepped outside. He took a deep breath and smiled as he inhaled the fresh sea air. Looking along the promenade, he noticed that it had already been decorated with colourful flags and images of the Burlamacco. He decided he would walk along the promenade after he had unpacked, and stepped back into his room.

Kevin had travelled light; just a small suitcase, and another case holding his camera equipment. He would take a few photographs to supplement his article. He was soon organised, and left the hotel, stepping out into the bright sunshine. He crossed the road over to the promenade and decided to go left. The promenade was not too busy as it was still early in the day. He strolled along, noting how all the upmarket shops, mostly clothes and jewellery stores, were each housed in its own individually designed building. For the weary shopper or walker, there were cafés and ice-cream parlours every so often.

He decided he was in need of a coffee, and stopped in front of a beautiful Art Nouveau building, by the name of 'Gran Caffe Margherita.' On the wall outside he noticed a plaque, and stepped closer to read what it said, taking out his notebook. He translated from the Italian and recorded the words in his notebook, for possible inclusion in his article later: 'And dear friends of the Maestro, from Italy and abroad, sat around this table that Giacomo Puccini had chosen as his meeting place to simply relax with some civil conversation after the extended efforts required by his Immortal Art'.

'I shall do as Puccini, and sit at the same table,' he thought. He ordered a cappuccino from the waiter standing by the door, then took out his camera from its case and started to take a few shots of the café and the view along the promenade. The coffee arrived with three small Italian biscuits on a plate. He thanked the waiter and jotted down a few further observations in his notebook.

As Kevin sipped his coffee, his attention turned to a group of about twenty boisterous young men, all dressed as Burlamacco, marching towards the café from the right side of the promenade. They followed an older man, similarly dressed, walking in front and carrying a flag. Kevin picked up his camera and started to take shots of the passing group, no doubt rehearsing for the big day tomorrow. They waved at him as they passed, and Kevin smiled, putting his thumb up in appreciation.

Soon they were followed by a long line of school children holding hands in twos, accompanied by their teachers. The children wore fancy dress costumes that they had probably made themselves, or had their parents make them. Finally a line of six elderly men approached, again dressed as Burlamacco, but with masks that were grotesque rather than the smiling ones the earlier group had been wearing. Kevin smiled at them too, and started to take more photographs. The group stopped as they passed the café, coming to a halt a few paces away.

The marchers stood still for a few seconds, making Kevin wonder why they had all suddenly stopped. He watched as the man at the back of the line turned his head to stare at him, making Kevin somewhat uncomfortable. He looked around, thinking the man was staring at someone or something else behind him; or perhaps at the couple on the next table, who were chatting and laughing. The man walked up to the table where Kevin was sitting. He stopped and stared, and the smile on Kevin's face wavered a little.

'You have a great costume!' said Kevin. He looked back up at the man, waiting for a response of some sort, but none came. How odd. What did the man want?

'I like the mask too. A bit scary, though'. Kevin gave a nervous laugh to try and break the ice. But again there was no response. The man looked down at the camera, then extended his hand and tapped on the palm with a finger of his other hand.

'What is it you want?' asked Kevin.

The man looked directly at Kevin and continued the hand movements.

'Is it money you want?' The man nodded his head in confirmation.

'For your photograph?' Kevin was getting annoyed now. The man again nodded his head.

'Be away with you, clown! I never pay for photographs!' said Kevin, waving him to go away.

The man stood motionless for a while, then turned and joined his group nearby. Kevin watched as they chatted for a few seconds amongst themselves. Then all six of the marchers turned their faces, covered by the grotesque masks, in his direction. He could see their eyes glaring at him through the slots in the masks, making him shudder. After a moment they turned their faces back in the direction they were travelling, and set off, following the other marchers, now in the distance.

Once they were all out of sight, Kevin looked around at the other tables. The couple next to him were still in their own world, as if nothing had happened, and most of the other tables were now full of tourists and locals, all equally oblivious. The waiter appeared at the door and Kevin asked for the bill, before paying and heading back in the direction of his hotel.

The promenade was busy with tourists and locals, some dressed in harlequin outfits, which slowed down his progress significantly. He crossed over to the other side of the promenade as it looked less busy, but soon that side became equally congested. He wanted to be back at the hotel as soon as possible. He started to feel agitated, and decided to turn into a side road that he knew would lead him to a parallel street to the "Passenggiata a Mare", hopefully not as crowded.

The side road was not congested at all. Only two people, dressed as tigers, passed him. As they did so, they raised their paws and growled at him jokingly. He increased his pace and turned into the parallel street. Kevin had calmed down by now, wiping sweat from his forehead, but continuing to walk at the same pace. For some reason, which he himself did not understand, he kept looking back over his shoulder ever so often to see if anyone was following him. No one was.

After 200 metres he turned into another side road that would lead him directly back to his hotel. He slowed his pace, breathing a sigh of relief. He noticed, a few paces ahead, several large pieces of cardboard stacked up against the door of a closed and dilapidated shop. As Kevin walked past he jumped when he saw the cardboard move; there was something behind. The first thing that came to mind was rats, so he stayed well away from the pile and observed from a distance. He instinctively took a photograph with the camera hanging around his neck. It was only when he saw a masked head appear that he realised it was actually a person behind all that cardboard, not rats.

Kevin approached to get a closer look and jumped again when a hand came out and grasped his ankle. He tried to shake the hand loose but couldn't, so he gave it a hard kick with his other foot. The person yelped and let go of Kevin's ankle, enabling him to move clear away. The cardboard collapsed, revealing an elderly man dressed as the familiar Burlamacco with a grotesque mask. He stretched out the palm of his hand up towards Kevin.

'Not another begging clown, you're all the same,' sneered Kevin. He pointed his camera at the man and took a few shots, thinking he would maybe have a small section in his article about the dark side of the carnival. Before Kevin left, he fished in his pocket and found a fifty cent coin and tossed it to the man.

Back in his hotel room, Kevin decided that he would write up some of the information he had collected that day, before going out to dinner. On his way out he stopped at reception, and asked for a restaurant recommendation.

'I can recommend Bar Trattoria Nostromo. My brother is the owner', said the lady behind reception, still dressed as Burlamacco, but without a mask. She then proceeded to explain what type of food was on offer, making Kevin think it was going to be expensive. But then, he wasn't too concerned at the cost as the newspaper would be paying.

'Would you like me to book a table for you?'

'Yes that would be great. Thank you.' The receptionist showed him on a map where the restaurant was, just a short walk from the hotel.

Kevin found it without difficulty. He ordered lobster as a starter with a glass of champagne, followed by a fillet steak washed down with an expensive bottle of red wine. For dessert he had a crêpe flambé. A most enjoyable meal, he thought to himself as he left the restaurant. He could get used to this.

He stood on the pavement outside, looking across the road at the same dilapidated shop as earlier. How could he have missed it when he had arrived at the restaurant? There was no cardboard outside now, and no sign of the strange man. Kevin wondered what had happened to him. Perhaps the police had moved him on. Anyway, it was not his problem, he decided, and headed back to the hotel.

The opening parade commenced at four o'clock the next day. Having spent most of the morning and early afternoon writing up the introduction for his article, he stepped outside onto his balcony and watched as the crowds built up, lining both sides of the "Passenggiata a Mare". Everywhere there were vendors selling food, drinks, and fancy costumes. Jugglers entertained the crowds waiting for the carnival procession to start. Music blared out from speakers all along the promenade. Soon in the distance Kevin saw the floats approaching, and the crowds started to cheer and wave flags. Accompanying the floats were marching bands and hundreds of dancers wearing colourful costumes of all sorts.

After several of the floats had passed his balcony, Kevin decided he would go down and join the crowds, and perhaps interview some of the spectators. Soon he was immersed in the music and dancing, and allowed himself to be carried along with the crowd. Colourful lights had come on all along the promenade as well as on the floats as the dancing and partying continued. He must have been enjoying himself so much that hours had flown past. the sun had set and it was getting dark.

Kevin spotted a large group dressed in the Burlamacco costume marching in front of a float, carrying an enormous figure of the mascot, made of papier-mâché. They turned their smiling masked faces and stared at him. Time seemed to have slowed down. Kevin looked around him and saw everyone was still dancing and cheering, but somehow it all seemed to be in slow motion. The group raised their arms and pointed at him. A low scream started emanating from the mouth openings of their masks, increasing in volume until the sound became deafening. Kevin put his hands to his ears and closed his eyes, and all of a sudden the screaming stopped.

He opened his eyes again. Everything was back to what it had been before; Kevin watched in wonder as the float passed by. Shaken by the experience he had just had, he turned to leave. It was time to head back to his hotel. As he started off he was surprised to find five men dressed as Burlamacco blocking his path. Their masks were not smiling. Kevin felt threatened, and immediately turned around and walked in the opposite direction as fast as he could, weaving through the dancing spectators. He glanced over his shoulder and saw the men following him, and upped his pace. He bumped into a crowd of people all dressed as fantastical creatures with horns, and tripped, falling on to the floor. He picked himself up and apologised to them profusely. They just laughed and continued dancing.

Kevin looked to see if the men were still hot on his trail. They were. He quickly turned into a side road, hoping they had not seen him, and started to run. He stopped half way up the road and looked back, panting heavily. The road was empty. Hoping he had lost them, he continued on his way, walking fast rather than running. He knew where he was going; it was the same route that he had taken the day before to avoid the crowds. No sooner had he turned the corner when he heard footsteps behind him. He looked back without stopping and started to run when he spotted two of the men behind him. They gave chase.

Kevin kept up the pace, knowing the road leading down to his hotel was not far ahead. He came to an abrupt stop when two more of the men appeared from that road. He looked across the street, and the fifth man appeared from a siding. What was he to do? He was trapped, and there was not a single spectator in sight to help him. What did they want?

He looked to his left and saw a gap between the buildings, an alleyway. He headed down it, as he had no other option. He could see the crowds at the end of the alleyway through a gate, and ran towards them. The men followed, close behind.

He got to the gate and pushed. It was locked. He held the grille with both hands and shook it, shouting for help. No one could hear him above the noise of the music and the cheering. No one could see him either, as they were all facing away, towards the floats on the promenade. Kevin sensed the men close by and turned to see them standing just behind him. He watched as they slowly pulled their masks up to reveal hideously deformed faces. His eyes widened and he opened his mouth to scream, but no sound came out. His knees gave way and he collapsed to the ground, looking up in horror at the men looming over him.

Kevin felt cold when he awoke. He must have passed out, he realised. He moved his neck from side to side. It was stiff. He was confused. When he moved his hands up to rub his face, he felt a mask there. He tried to prise it off, but it was firmly fixed to his face. He could just see a soft light through the eye slots of the mask, and when he opened his eyes fully he was able to see daylight through a small gap in front of him. He was underneath something, but he was not sure what it was. He tried to stand up, but the muscles in his legs would not work. In the attempt, whatever he was covered by fell away. He saw large sheets of cardboard on either side of him, and, looking down, he realised he was wearing the outfit of The Burlamacco.

Just then a man appeared in front of him. Kevin reached out and grabbed the man's ankle. The man instinctively shook his leg to get away then kicked Kevin's hand with the other foot. With a yelp he let go. Kevin raised his other hand towards the man, asking assistance to help him to his feet. He tried to speak but no words materialised.

The man took hold of the camera that was hanging around his neck and started to take photographs of him lying amongst the cardboard. Instead of helping Kevin up, the man shouted something, and tossed a coin at him before leaving, without looking back.

THE CURSE OF THE SHABTI

Professor Crispin Scarpia sat in a director's chair, his eagle eyes watching as the assistant curators of the Archaeology Museum of Bologna put the finishing touches to his upcoming exhibition. He was immaculately dressed in a tweed suit, and held on to his ornate silver topped walking cane with both hands. Everyone clapped and cheered as a huge banner was hoisted up at the entrance to the Exhibition Hall - all except for Dr Luisa Becatti, the chief archaeologist and curator of the museum. She studied Professor Scarpia's face from a distance, waiting to see how he would react to the completion of his project.

Throughout the duration of the setup, Professor Scarpia would arrive early in the Exhibition Hall and sit in his chair, waiting for the assistant curators to commence their tasks. Every day he would present Dr Becatti a sheet of his personal headed notepaper, on which he had written an exhaustive list of criticisms of the way her staff were setting up the exhibits. She had never before had to work with such a perfectionist as Professor Scarpia, who micromanaged everything they did. She would have challenged him if it weren't for the fact that he was best pals with the Trustees, and had donated large sums of money to the museum.

Luisa watched as he stood up with the aid of his cane and strolled over to the glass exhibit cases, clutching a notepad and gold pen. He peered at the Egyptian artefacts over the top of his glasses and, as usual, started to make notes. Her stomach sank at the thought that he had found something else to criticise. She gripped her hands together tightly and glanced at her staff, who were all silent now, also watching the professor. One of them gave her a quick supportive smile and she nodded her head in appreciation.

The Exhibition Hall was silent except for the sound of Professor Scarpia's footsteps echoing as he walked over to the next cabinet. This one contained a collection of about thirty shabtis, Egyptian funerary figurines in the form of small figures, placed in an ancient tomb to do any work that the dead person might be called upon to do in the afterlife. Luisa was not surprised that he spent an inordinately long time studying them, as the shabtis were the highlight of the exhibition, in particular one made of blue faience; much bigger than the others, it was a very rare piece. The display notes pointed out that it was the only one of its kind. Luisa's stomach sank again when he shook his head from side to side and wrote something in his pad.

At last he finished reviewing the display cabinets, and she was relieved that he had not made any more additions to his notebook. He strolled over to her and gave her a weak smile before speaking.

'There is a mistake on the notes to the blue shabti, which I would like you to correct before the opening of the exhibition,' he said looking at his notepad.

'I am so sorry, Professor Scarpia. What is the mistake?'

'The height of the shabti is written as 20cm. It should of course read 20.5cm.'

'I will have it amended immediately.' Luisa turned and gave instructions to one of her staff, who promptly went off to deal with the matter.

'Is there anything else, professor?' asked Luisa. She held her breath.

'No, that is all. We can go ahead with the official opening tomorrow.' Professor Scarpia closed his note pad, picked up his coat from the back of his chair and his hat from the nearby table, and headed out of the Exhibition Hall. Luisa let out a sigh of relief as her staff came over to congratulate her.

The professor made his way out of the museum and headed to the house that he had been renting for the past year. He had arrived in Bologna directly from the excavation site he was helping to fund, in the Theban Necropolis on the west bank of the Nile at Luxor. Professor Scarpia had concluded that the tomb that he had found was that of a high ranking official or prince during the reign of the pharaoh Seti I, although the evidence was not so far conclusive. The burial chamber itself, where the coffin of the mummy would have been, had still not been found by the time he had to leave Egypt in a hurry due to the worsening political situation. It was too dangerous for him to stay and continue the excavation.

All the artefacts, in particular the shabtis, that Professor Scarpia and his team had found in the first chamber of the tomb had been boxed up in crates, destined for the Cairo Museum. At the last minute, worried about their safety, the professor had decided to take them to Alexandria instead. He had liberally bribed the lorry drivers and various officials, and in the ensuing chaos, the items were successfully shipped to Italy. Professor Scarpia was no thief, however. He fully intended to return everything back to Egypt once the country was stable again, and he could be sure of the safety of his precious finds.

The housekeeper, Arianna, was busy dusting the hallway as he entered. 'Good afternoon, Professor Scarpia. I hope you've had a successful day at the museum.'

'I most certainly have, Arianna, thank you.'

She indicated his hat and coat. 'Let me take those.'

The professor took his hat and coat off, and handed them to her.

'I'll prepare lunch. You go and warm yourself by the fire in the reception room.'

Arianna hung his coat up and placed the hat on the small table by the door, then started to make her way to the kitchen. Remembering something, she stopped and delved into the pocket at the front of her apron, extracting a letter.

'This came for you while you were out.' She handed the letter to the professor, then disappeared into the kitchen at the back of the hallway.

Professor Scarpia looked at the letter. It only had his name on the front and nothing else. He turned it over to see if the name or address of the sender was on the back, but there was only a small red wax seal. He made his way into the reception room, poured himself a sherry, then sat down in a tall-backed leather armchair in front of a roaring log fire. He took a sip of the sherry then placed the glass on a side table and broke the wax sealing the envelope.

He was surprised to find a piece of papyrus paper, folded in half. He smoothed it out and read the contents.

'Dear Professor Crispin Scarpia,

You do not know us, but we have followed the progress of your excavation from the moment you discovered the Tomb of Nefermenu. We have a warning for you. Return the shabtis to their rightful owner before it is too late. We can arrange for their safe passage back to Egypt. The exhibition must not go ahead. We mean you no harm. We will be waiting for you outside the museum at 5pm tonight.

He turned the letter over to check the back in case there was anything else written there. It was blank. He refolded the papyrus sheet and placed it back in the envelope, then picked up his glass and sipped the sherry, musing over the contents of the letter.

The shabtis belonged to him. He was the one who had found them and brought them to a safe haven in Italy. He had no doubt they would have been lost, stolen or destroyed in the ongoing conflict if he had left them in Egypt.

They will stay in Bologna, and the exhibition will go ahead as planned, he said to himself. He finished his sherry, and still clutching the letter, stood up in front of the open fire and tossed the letter into it. He watched as it burst into flames, disintegrating to black fragments that wafted up the chimney and were soon gone. Just then Arianna entered the room and informed him that lunch was ready to be served in the dining room.

'Arianna, did you see the person who delivered that letter? Or was it just posted through the letterbox?

'It was posted through the letterbox. But as I was opening the dining room curtains this morning, I did see a man leave. I couldn't see his face, but I noticed he was wearing what looked like Arabic attire.'

'I see,' said Professor Scarpia, looking back at the fireplace.

After lunch, Arianna cleared the plates and said she was going out for a few hours to visit her mother. Once she had left, the professor yawned and decided he would have an afternoon siesta. Wearily holding his walking stick, he climbed the stairs and slumped onto his bed. It did not take long for him to fall asleep.

He drifted in and out of sleep, awakening suddenly when he heard the wooden stairs creaking. He assumed it was Arianna coming back from visiting her mother.

'Is that you, Arianna?' he called. No answer came.

He heard the stairs creak again, but the sound seemed much closer this time. A scraping noise came from the left side of the bed.

'Oh no! We must have mice,' he said to himself. He was too tired to take a look. The scraping noises continued, now coming from under the bed.

'There must be a whole family of them. I'll get Arianne to put some poison down.'

He rolled over onto his side and, picking up his walking stick, reached under the bed and hit the floorboards to scare the creatures away. The sound of scraping stopped.

He rolled onto his back again and froze, dropping his walking stick, which clattered to the floor. At the end his iron bed stood a figure, an Egyptian mummy, covered in ripped dirty bandages and holding its arms directly out to him.

Professor Scarpia wanted to get up and run from the room, but was transfixed on the bed, unable to move, staring at the creature. His face twisted in horror as he watched the mummy's slit of a mouth open wide as if to speak, then he screamed as it disgorged flying shabtis at him, landing all over him, covering him completely.

'What is the matter, professor? Are you all right?'

Professor Scarpia opened his eyes to see Arianne standing over him. She helped to lift him up to a sitting position as he wiped perspiration from his forehead. His heart was racing and he held his palms against his chest.

'Shall I call a doctor?' said Arianne, worried that he was having a heart attack.

'No. No. I am fine. It was just a nightmare.'

'Are you sure?' she insisted.

'Yes. I am fine. Thank you. Please go. I am sure you have things to do.'

Arianne reluctantly left him and went downstairs. His breathing and heartbeat gradually returned to normal, and he got out of bed and followed her down.

'I think we have mice. I heard them under the bed. Could you please buy some poison next time you go out?'

'Are you sure, professor? I haven't seen any. But I'll get some poison and put it down, if you like, to be sure.'

Professor Scarpia decided he needed to get out of the house and go for a walk to clear his mind. He picked up his coat from the coat rack by the door, collected his hat, and told Arianna that he would not require supper that evening. He thought he would contact a friend and dine out.

He headed in the direction of the Archaeology Museum, stopping outside for a brief moment to look at the large banner promoting his exhibition. He noticed crowds of people leaving from the front entrance and pulled out his pocket watch. It was 5pm and the museum was closing for the day. Once the crowds had cleared, he saw three figures standing at the entrance, looking in his direction. The tallest man was dressed in Arabic attire, flanked on either side by burly men dressed in black suits. Professor Scarpia thought back to the contents of the letter he had been handed that morning, and started to walk briskly away from the museum towards the nearby Piazza Maggiore.

On the way he phoned his friend, Professor Edwards, who taught Classics at Bologna University. He arranged to meet him at 6pm at the Signorvino wine bar on the Piazza. As soon as he had finished the call, he looked back over his shoulder and noticed the three men had gone. He had half expected them to be following him.

He turned right into a crowded narrow street, the Via Pescherie Vecchie, lined with bars, restaurants and delicatessens, and walked slowly, taking his time to observe all the delicious foods and drinks that were on offer. At the end of the road he turned right, then right again, and headed back towards Piazza Maggiore. He passed a small crowd that had gathered around a man playing an accordion and a young woman dancing to the music. The crowd applauded and tossed coins into the hat that the woman offered around when they ended their performance.

As the crowd dispersed, Professor Scarpia was surprised to see the three men again, who were now surely following him. Feeling somewhat uneasy, he hurriedly walked away. He looked back at the men, noticing they had upped their pace to match his. The street had become quieter, and he could hear their footsteps behind him, getting closer and closer.

He was relieved when he could see the Piazza thronged with people ahead. He took one last glance back at his pursuers, and immediately crashed into someone.

'My apologies, sir. How clumsy of me!' said Professor Scarpia.

'I should say so, professor!' The man said, laughing.

'Oh, it's you, John! Professor Scarpia had bumped into Professor Edwards.

'Well, Crispin, fancy that.' Professor Edwards extended his hand. They shook, and Professor Scarpia looked behind him to see if the men were still hot on his trail. They had disappeared.

'Who's chasing you, then? said Professor Edwards, following the direction of his gaze.

'Oh, nobody. It's nothing.'

'Really?' Professor Edwards was not convinced.

'Are you hurt? Professor Scarpia asked as an afterthought.

'I'm fine, but I could do with a drink.'

'Come on then, let me buy you one. I know a nice little bar nearby. In fact, there it is,' said Professor Scarpia. He led his friend by the arm towards the establishment.

Later, over dinner, they discussed Professor Scarpia's upcoming exhibition, and how he had discovered the artefacts. No mention was made of the letter he had received, or the three men following him. At the end of the evening, the two men went off in opposite directions, and although it was only a short distance back to his house, Professor Scarpia walked briskly, all the time having the feeling he was being followed. On reaching his house, he entered quickly without looking back.

He read for a while, until his eyes were too tired to continue. Before he switched out the lights, curiosity got the better of him, and he got out of bed and went over to the window. He moved the curtain aside slightly, and peered out onto the street below. Somehow he wasn't surprised to see three figures standing by a closed cafe a little distance away. The faint light just about illuminated their faces, and he could see the whites of their eyes staring up at him. He was glad he had double locked the door and checked all the windows before he had come up. He let the curtain fall, and went back to bed.

The early morning rays of sun shone through a gap in the curtains, awaking Professor Scarpia. He yawned and rubbed his eyes, reaching for his glasses lying on the bedside table. He felt fully refreshed from an uninterrupted night of sleep, devoid of nightmares or strange noises coming from under his bed. Arianna must have put the rat poison down.

He smiled at himself in the bathroom mirror as he prepared himself for the grand opening of his exhibition. After a quick breakfast, he headed out to the museum, arriving an hour before it was due to open. He was met by Dr Luisa Becatti at the staff entrance.

'Good morning, professor.'

'Good morning!' He thought she had a worried look on her face.

'We have a problem, professor.'

He frowned. 'What problem?'

'Follow me, and I'll explain.' They made their way to an office on the first floor, with the name Professor Bellini on the door. Dr Becatti knocked twice, then opened the door. Professor Scarpia gasped, for there, sitting in front of the desk, were the three men who had been following him.

'Come in, professor!' said a voice he recognised. He entered the room and saw the Chairman of the museum standing to the right of the doorway, by a glass bookshelf.

'Good morning, Professor Bellini. May I ask what is going on?'

'Take a seat and I will explain.' The three men already sitting watched as he made himself comfortable on a chair by the window.

'This is Dr Omar Hadad and his colleagues Mr Nazari and Mr Kassab, from the Egyptian Museum in Cairo.' They all smiled at Professor Scarpia. He gave a weak smile in return, still somewhat wary of the trio. These were the men who had been following him, and the ones that had sent him the letter, he presumed. Dr Hadad spoke first.

'I hope you received and read the letter from us.'

'Yes, I did.'

'Then you know that the exhibition cannot open.'

'Why not?' Professor Scarpia looked to Professor Bellini.

'I have this signed request from the Egyptian Antiquities Minister.' Professor Bellini picked up a document from the table and presented it to Professor Scarpia.

'It states that all the artefacts in your exhibition are the property of the Egyptian Nation, illegally taken out of the country. They must be returned immediately,' said Dr Hadad.

'Nonsense. I was the one who found them. Without me they would have been lost, or even destroyed.

You can't stop my exhibition opening. I will not allow it!

'Calm down, Crispin. Perhaps you should have a coffee and let me deal with this. Dr Becatti, would you please accompany Professor Scarpia to the cafeteria? I will join you both shortly.'

'Certainly. This way, professor,' said Dr Becatti. Professor Scarpia reluctantly got up from his chair and followed her out of the room. She closed the door behind them.

A short while later, Professor Scarpia saw Dr Hadad and his colleagues walk past the cafe on their way out of the museum. Professor Bellini appeared and sat next to him. He smiled.

'Good news! I managed to convince Dr Hadad to allow the exhibition to open today and run for a week, after which we will need to box up all the artefacts and return them.'

' Is that the best you can do? A week is nothing.' Professor Scarpia looked defeated.

' Sorry Crispin, I'm afraid so. You're going to have to bite the bullet on this one, old friend, otherwise the Egyptian Government will kick up a huge fuss. It's too big a price to pay. You have been a little naughty, you know.'

Professor Scarpia thought for a while, then smiled in resignation. At least there was still going to be an exhibition, and tickets would be like gold dust.

By 9.00am a long queue of visitors had already built up outside as the doors to the museum opened, eager to see the exhibition. By closing time everyone was elated. It had been a great success. A small party was held at the museum that evening, attended by Professor Scarpia, Professor Bellinin and Dr Becatti and her staff. Also in attendance were Dr Hadad and his team, as well as several officials from the Mayor's office.

Professor Scarpia gave a short speech, gracefully thanking Mr Hadad for allowing him to display the artefacts from the tomb. He also thanked Dr Becatti and her team setting up the exhibition.

One week later the exhibition closed as agreed, and Professor Scarpia supervised the crating up of the artefacts with Dr Hadad in attendance. The last crate to be packed held the shabtis. The rare blue one was the last to be put in.

'May I just hold it one more time before it is packed?' Professor Scarpia said to the assistant curator who was carefully positioning it. The curator handed it over, and he held the shabti carefully in both hands. He held it close to his chest and noticed Dr Hadad walk over to a closed crate nearby, where he was asked to sign travel documents relating to it by a member of staff. Professor Scarpia turned back to the open crate in front of him and waited for Dr Hadad to return. When he did, he gently placed the blue shabti into the foam packaging before the crate was nailed shut. Dr Hadad signed the documents relating to it and watched as it was lifted by two burly museum employees and carried out to the truck waiting outside.

Dr Hadad and Professor Scarpia shook hands at the entrance to the museum. He watched as Dr Hadad and his team climbed into a black limousine and followed the truck out of the museum gates.

When Professor Scarpia reached his house, he went straight up to his bedroom. Arianna watched him, thinking it strange that he had not taken his overcoat off. He entered the bedroom and carefully closed and locked the door. Then he reached inside his coat and pulled out an object. He held it in front of his face and smiled. It was the blue faience shabti.

'Beautiful shabti. You are mine now. I found you, and you will be mine forever,' he whispered. How clever he had been, arranging for a local potter in Egypt to make a copy before he left. They were so skilled at replicas, it was almost impossible to tell the difference. When everyone, including Dr Hadad, had been preoccupied, he had simply swapped the original for the copy, placing it in the spacious inside pocket of his overcoat.

As a precaution, Professor Scarpia had decided to hide the blue shabti until he was due to leave Bologna in a few days time, in the unlikely event that Dr Hadad discovered in the meantime that the one in his possession was a fake. When he was sure that Arianne had gone, he went out into the garden, where an outhouse contained various implements and tools. He selected a few that he could use to lift one of the floorboards under the bed.

Having successfully done so, he wrapped the blue shabti in one of his silk scarves and carefully placed it in the gap. Then he re-nailed the floorboard securely in place. He would retrieve it when he was ready to leave. He replaced the tools back in the garden outhouse, and returned to his room.

He took his coat and Jacket off and placed them on a nearby chair, then sat on the bed. He yawned and stretched his arm out, and feeling suddenly exhausted, he lay down, closing his eyes. Sleep came instantly.

A smell of something burning assailed his nostrils. He opened his eyes and gasped when he saw that the room was filled with smoke. His immediate thought was that the house was on fire, and he quickly got out of bed. His heart was beating rapidly as he stumbled to the closed door and opened it.

He froze. He was looking out on to a long hall, lined with statues of Egyptian gods; human figures with the heads of cats, crocodiles and jackals. A path led to a set of steps, leading up to a podium of some sort, but he couldn't see what was on it, as it was obscured by gauze curtains, gently wafting. The smoke, he realised, was in fact incense, burning in metal cauldrons in front of each of the statues. The sweet smell was quite overpowering.

I must be dreaming, he thought to himself. He pinched his arm, hard. He felt the pain. He turned around and saw the bedroom he had come out of had disappeared, only a dark entrance remaining to be seen.

A loud deep voice boomed from the direction of the podium. He did not understand the words at first; it was in a language at once foreign but somehow familiar. Then suddenly he found that he knew what they were saying.

'Come forward, Professor Scarpia!'

'Who is it? How do you name my name?'

'Come forward!' The voice reverberated around the hall.

Something took control of Professor Scarpia's legs and he reluctantly placed one foot in front of the other, approaching the podium as he had been commanded. The first set of curtains parted as he reached the first step. He started to ascend, and another curtain was pulled back in front. There were men dressed as Ancient Egyptians standing either side, holding the curtains. The final set were pulled back to reveal a man sitting on a throne, dressed in the formal attire of a nobleman of Ancient Egypt.

The man was surrounded by others, some holding trays laden with food, others drink. A tall slim man held out a tray to the man on the throne. It held a golden goblet and a golden jug. Another man took hold of the jug and poured a red liquid into the goblet, presenting it to the sitting man.

'Who are you? Asked Professor Scarpia.

'I am Nefermenu, Chief advisor to the Pharaoh.'

'This isn't real. I'm still dreaming. Aren't I?' Professor Scarpia looked down to his chest and arms. He was also wearing Egyptian attire. He had not noticed until now.

'No, Professor. You are not dreaming. You are really here, in my presence.'

'Where is here?' he asked, expecting to wake up any moment.

'You would call it the afterlife...'

'No. No! This isn't real. Wake up. Wake up!' Professor Scarpia pinched himself again, harder.

'You took the blue shabti from my tomb for your personal pleasure. You never intended to return it to Egypt. So now, you must serve me in its place for all eternity!'

Professor Scarpia held his head with his hands and screamed.

***

'I thought something was odd when the professor came home and went upstairs with his winter coat on,' said Arianne to Professor Edwards. She was crying into her handkerchief. They watched as a doctor examined Professor Scarpia lying on the bed.

'How did he die, Doctor?' asked Professor Edwards.

'A heart attack, I'm afraid.'

'What about his face? When I found him, he looked like he was terrified of something,' said Arianne.

'Yes, sometimes that can happen, especially when the attack is swift and fatal.'

The doctor packed away his equipment. Two orderlies arrived with a stretcher and took away the body to a waiting ambulance.

Professor Edwards followed the doctor out of the room. Arianne closed the door, unaware that beneath the bed, under the floorboards, lay the blue shabti.

Perhaps someone will find it one day and it can be returned to Egypt, releasing Professor Scarpia from his eternal servitude.

Or perhaps not.

CASTELLO BARTOLO

They had met outside the La Gritta restaurant in Portofino. Rachael was on holiday with three of her university friends, celebrating their final year results. They had all passed with flying colours and were looking forward to pursuing their chosen careers. Rachael had studied for a degree in Fine Art and had already secured an internship with The National Gallery in London, which she would start on her return to the UK.

'I'm going for a walk to explore the town. Who would like to join me?' asked Sarah, one of Rachael's friends.

'I will!' said Peter.

'How about you two?' Sarah raised a quizzical eyebrow at Rachael and Simon.

'I'm quite content sitting here and sipping my wine, but you go, Simon,' said Rachael.

'Are you sure you are going to be fine sitting here on your own? asked Simon.

'Yes, I'll be perfectly fine. Now go!' She gave him a friendly smile. Rachael and Simon had dated each other since they had met during the first year of their degree course, but had ended their relationship a few months ago to concentrate on their final exams. They remained good friends.

Rachael watched as her three friends walked along the side of the harbour heading to the nearby piazza, taking snaps with their phones. They posed for a group selfie by a red painted rowing boat, then continued along the opposite side of the harbour towards a botanical garden interspersed with art installations. She turned around to catch the eye of the waiter and ordered another glass of wine. In so doing, she noticed a tall man wearing a smart blazer and red trousers pulling up the wooden shutters of the building next to the restaurant. She continued to watch as he secured the shutters, then brushed the dark hair on his head back before unlocking the door and entering what was now revealed to be a shop.

She looked up at the shop's name. ' Alfonso Portofino Gallery'. How exciting, she thought to herself, and decided she would pay the Gallery a visit once she had finished her wine - which arrived at that instant.

She took a sip and glanced across to the other side of the harbour to see if her friends were still visible, but she couldn't see them. They must have gone into the botanical gardens, she decided. Rachel changed seats so that she was facing the art Gallery, and noticed the man she had seen earlier was moving around the paintings in the shop window. He took two of them out and replaced them with others. She could not see his face, as it was obscured by a window blind that had not been fully pulled up. All she could see were his hands.

She was curious to see the paintings he had put in the window. Maybe they were within her budget, and she could purchase one as a souvenir to remind her of Portofino. She was also a little curious about the shopkeeper himself. Rachel finished her glass of wine and called the waiter over to settle the bill, which included the drinks her friends had consumed. Her eyes widened when she saw how expensive the drinks were, but tried not to show it. She took the money out of the general kitty that she was in charge of, and smiled at the waiter, telling him to keep the change. She then texted her friends to let them know where she would be in case they came back to the restaurant looking for her.

Rachael picked up her wide brimmed hat and put it on, then walked over to the Gallery shop. She glanced at the paintings, noticing her reflection on the glass window of the shop, and adjusted her hat slightly. How chic she looked, she thought, smiling at her own reflection.

The paintings were all of a high standard. She looked out for price tags, but none were visible. They are probably way above my budget, she thought, especially as the Gallery was situated in one of the priciest parts of Italy.

One particular painting caught her attention and she moved closer until her nose was almost touching the glass. It was a dramatic painting of a cliff top castle during a storm, showing the waves crashing against the rocks at the shoreline. The lights of the castle were on which gave it a sense of cosiness and safety in the storm, but the more she studied it the more that feeling melted away to be replaced by a feeling of danger. Despite the hot weather outside she felt the light hairs on her arms stand on end and felt a sudden chill.

The shop door suddenly opened, accompanied by the sound of a tinkling bell. The man she saw earlier, who had opened up the Gallery, appeared. He took out a cigarette from a golden case and placed it in his mouth, clipping the case shut, then took out a silver lighter from his pocket and lit the cigarette. He took a deep, satisfying drag, closing his eyes, exhaling the smoke slowly into the air, lifting his chin up as he did so. Then he turned and smiled at Rachael.

'Good afternoon,' he said, in a deep rich tone. For a moment Rachael was stunned by his deep blue eyes and chiselled handsome face.

'Good afternoon.' Rachael felt herself blushing, having stared at him for far too long, she thought, before answering. She watched as he took another long drag from his cigarette.

'Do you like the paintings you're looking at?' He spoke without looking at her, instead staring to the other side of the harbour.

'Yes! They are amazing. Of such high quality. Especially that one.' Rachael turned and pointed at the painting of the cliff top castle in the storm.

'That is one of my favourites, too.'

'Really?' Rachael turned back to the shopkeeper. 'I'm glad we agree.'

'How rude of me not to introduce myself. I am Alfonso di Bartolo. And your name?'

'Rachael. My name is Rachael. I'm here with my friends. They have gone sightseeing...sorry, I'm twittering now.'

'It is a pleasure to meet you, Rachael,' said Alfonso, extending his hand. They shook hands. Rachel turned red again, and felt somewhat embarrassed.

'Would you like a closer look at the painting?

'Yes, I would, but I imagine it is way beyond my price range.'

'Come inside and have a look at it anyway.' Alfonso dropped his cigarette on the floor, stamped on it, then picked it up and put it into a nearby public bin.

Rachael followed him into the Gallery shop. Alfonso took the painting from the window and gently passed it over to her. He watched her intensely as she studied the painting.

'What attracts you to this particular painting, might I ask?'

'I just love the way the artist has painted the waves crashing onto the rocks, so dynamic, and it has such a sense of realism. The scene is almost moving before your eyes, especially the storm clouds rolling in, and I love the cosiness of the castle perched high up on the cliff top, safe from the chaos below.' Rachael looked up at Alfonso.

'Very well observed. You seem knowledgeable on the subject of art.'

'Well, yes, I do know a bit about it. In fact I have just graduated in Fine Art from a university in London.' Rachael was trying her best not to boast.

'That is impressive,' said Alfonso. Rachael noticed him studying her face intensely with his stunning blue eyes. He hardly blinked, making her look away and blush again. She glanced down at the lower corners of the painting looking for the artist's signature, but could not see one.

'I think we passed this castle on our way here. I got a glimpse of it through some trees as we came around one of the sharp bends on the coastal road. It's an amazing building. I wonder who lives there. Do you know?' asked Rachael, looking up from the painting. Alfonso did not answer for what seemed a long time as he gazed directly into her eyes. The incredible blueness of them held her in a hypnotic trance, until at last they were interrupted by the tinkling bell. The shop door opened and in walked her three friends.

'There you are, Rachael! We thought we'd lost you,' said Sarah.

'Didn't you get my text?

'No, we didn't.' They all consulted their phones. Simon and Peter shook their heads.

'Never mind. You found me.' Rachael was a little annoyed that her friends had interrupted her concentration.

'So who's this fine gentleman, then?' asked Sarah, looking Alfonso up and down with great interest. He noticed, and moved forward to introduce himself.

'I am Alfonso di Bartolo, the owner of the Gallery.' He took hold of her hand and kissed the top.

'I'm Sarah. Pleased to meet you.' She giggled and gave him a short curtsy.

'I am pleased to meet you, too.'

'What a perfect gentlemen!' said Sarah turning to Rachael. Rachael glared at her and took hold of

Alfonso's arm, leading him away to meet the boys, much to his surprise.

'And these are my friends Simon and Peter.' Alfonso greeted them with a hand shake. Rachael detected an element of jealousy coming from Simon, whereas Peter stared at his eyes, entranced by their blueness.

'I was just showing Rachael this painting of my home, Castello Bartolo, that I completed a few months ago,' said Alfonso, making Rachael gasp.

'You painted this? And it's your castle?'

'That's what he just said, Rachael.'

She turned to a smiling Sarah and glared at her again. 'Why don't you all meet me outside for another drink. I won't be long.'

'We get the hint. Come on you two, let's leave Rachael to her artist friend', said Simon.

'He's not my friend, we've only just met.' She gave them the 'get lost' look that they were all too familiar with. They laughed, but promptly exited the Gallery shop and strolled to find a wine bar that was hopefully not as expensive as the restaurant next door.

'Sorry about my friends.'

'No need to apologise! Friends are friends,' said Alfonso laughing.

'Have you been an artist for long?' asked Rachael.

'All my life, yes.'

'Would you mind if I saw some of your other work?' she asked.

He thought for a few seconds. 'Come this way. I would like to know your opinion of this painting.' Rachael followed him to the counter at the back of the Gallery where a full length portrait of a young woman stood against the wall. She was standing by a tall blue Chinese vase with pink and red peonies in full bloom set on an antique marble table. The woman was dressed in a red evening gown with a short trail, and held a cocktail glass with a clear liquid inside, which she presumed was a gin martini. Rachael noticed the ornate necklace she was wearing, which looked as if it was studded with diamonds and rubies.

The more she looked at the painting the more she thought that something was not quite right about it. The face of the woman looked modern, and did not really fit with the surroundings, which consisted of old oak wood panelling, giving a sense of great age. Rachael guessed that the woman was in her mid twenties. Her face had a beautiful sereneness about it, apart from her eyes, which seemed somehow to tell a different story.

'What do you think? asked Alfonso.

'It's a skilfully executed painting, and I like the way the artist contrasts the modern and traditional aspects. I like it very much!' She was not totally honest.

'I'm glad you like it...' Alfonso was about to continue when Rachael interrupted.

'Is it one of yours?' she asked.

'Yes.'

'Is she your wife?' It was a wild guess, and very upfront of her to suggest it. She hated to admit it to herself, but in the short time she had been in the Gallery, Alfonso had ticked all the boxes as a potential boyfriend. She had to find out if he was married. He turned and walked to the front of the shop without speaking and gazed out of the shop window. Rachael closed her eyes, thinking that she had totally blown it. Any minute now he was going to ask her to leave the shop.

'No, she is not my wife. I am not married,' he said. Rachael felt like jumping for joy, but did her best to suppress the urge, hoping he had not noticed. His next words totally surprised her, and she allowed herself to think she was definitely in with a chance.

'I have a proposition for you. I am not sure how much longer you are staying in Portofino, but I would like you to be my model for a painting. I don't expect an answer immediately. By all means go away and think about it, and let me know tomorrow. I will remunerate you, of course.'

'Yes! I'd love to!' Rachael was taken aback by his offer, but she answered without thinking.

'Excellent!'

Rachael reconsidered her almost indecent haste. 'Well, I mean... maybe yes. As long as the modelling is not nude, or...' Alfonso laughed.

'No need to worry about that, Rachael. You will be attired just as in the painting you have just seen.'

'Really?' She turned and looked at the painting of the woman wearing the red gown again.

'I will pay you 5,000 Euros as a fee. Is that enough?'

'5,000 Euros!' Rachael gasped at the amount.

'I am sorry. I have offended you. Perhaps 10,000 Euros is a better figure.'

'No! Err... 5,000 is fine. Excuse me, I'd better go and tell my friends.' Rachael headed towards the exit, all flustered.

'I would like to start tomorrow, if that is fine with you. We can meet here tomorrow at 10am, or I can pick you up from your hotel.'

'Yes, ok... Here tomorrow is fine. I'd better go before my friends get annoyed that I made them wait so long.' Alfonso followed her to the door and opened it, standing aside to let her exit.

'See you tomorrow,' he said.

'Yes, see you tomorrow.' Rachael left the Gallery and almost shouted out with excitement. She couldn't wait to tell her friends about her good fortune. Not only was she going to make a lot of money, but there was also the chance to have some romance.

Alfonso lit another cigarette and took a drag as he watched Rachael cross the piazza towards a wine bar, where she could see her friends sitting outside at a table under a large white parasol. He continued watching the group until he finished the cigarette, and then threw the butt into the sea, before disappearing into his Gallery.

Rachael excitedly explained to her friends the offer made by Alfonso, and how fortunate she had been to meet him.

'He's very handsome, Rachael. I think you may have hit the jackpot there. I am sooooo jealous!' said Sarah.

'Are you sure you can trust him? You're not being sold into white slavery?' said Simon.

'You're not the only one who's jealous, Sarah,' said Peter. They all laughed, except Simon.

'I'm serious Rachael. Who offers you 5,000 Euros for a portrait just like that?'

'Mr Alfonso does, and he lives in a castle. I am totally flattered he wants to paint me, to be honest, and pay me 5,000 Euros for the privilege. I can pay a big chunk off of my university debt. I still can't believe my good fortune!'

'Don't let it go to your head and muddle up your thoughts. Are you 100% sure about this?' asked Simon, genuinely concerned about her safety.

'Yes! I trust him 100%, Simon. Well maybe 99%.'

'And maybe a little bit of romance?' said Sarah, raising her eyebrows.

'I'm counting on it!' They all burst out in laughter again, except for Simon. Rachael put her arm around him and again reassured him it was all fine. He eventually came around and joined in the joyous banter.

Over further glasses of wine in the evening before dinner, the three friends decided that they would check up on Rachael at regular intervals by phone to make sure she was fine, while she was having her portrait painted. She agreed, but insisted that they didn't phone more than every couple of hours. She didn't want all three of them phoning her on the hour, every hour as she was posing for the painting, interrupting the concentration of Alfonso.

Having dined well, they returned to their hotel rooms. When Rachael was alone in her room, she started having second thoughts about the next day. She considered what Simon had said. Was Alfonso's offer too good to be true? Did he have an ulterior motive in wanting to paint her? He was offering her 5,000 Euros for the privilege... Rachael let the pros and cons of his intentions move in and out of her thoughts, and finally resolved she would go ahead and act as a model for his painting.

They met as agreed the next day, while her friends took the local bus to visit the nearby seaside resort of Santa Margherta Ligure.

'We will use the studio at the back of the Gallery,' said Alfonso. He opened an opaque glass door that lead into a vast room with tall windows, allowing the light to flood in.

'Who will look after the shop, while you are engaged in your work?' asked Rachael. She was a little concerned that the front door would be locked.

'I have my assistant working here today. She will look after any customers who come in.' Just then the door bells tinkled, and a woman dressed in an immaculate yellow suit with matching yellow gloves and handbag entered the shop.

'Bongiorno, Signor Alfonso!'

'Bongiorno, Signorina Isabella. Let me introduce La Signorina Rachael. She will be modelling for me today.' The woman peered at Rachael over her sixties style spectacles as she took her gloves off. Then she walked up to Rachael and extended her left hand. Rachael instinctively extended her right hand, then realising it was awkward, used her left to shake hands.

'It's a pleasure to meet you,' Isabella said, and turned her head to Alfonso. Rachael sensed that they were communicating without saying a word. She watched as Isabella walked over to a nearby desk and started tidying up some glossy art magazines that were sitting there. She opened various draws and extracted notebooks and folders, before settling on the chair behind the desk facing the entrance to the Gallery. Here she could see any customers coming in.

'I am not to be disturbed until noon, unless it is extremely urgent, Signorina Isabella.'

'I'll make sure you are not, Signor Alfonso.' She peered at Rachael again over the top of her spectacles, making Rachael feel somewhat uncomfortable, then looked back down at what she was doing. What did she think was going to happen in the studio? thought Rachael. All Alfonso was going to do was to paint her.

'Come this way.' They entered the studio and Alfonso closed the door behind them. He took a white artist's apron from a rack by the door and put it on. It was already covered in paint of various colours. It did not take her long to spot the red evening gown hanging from a free standing rack across the room. Rachael made her way to it and felt the material with her fingers.

'This is beautiful,' she said, realising that it was identical to the one she had seen in the painting against the wall outside in the Gallery. Alfonso, in the mean time, set up a large easel in the middle of the room. He selected a blank canvas from the several stacked against the wall and placed it on the easel.

'Do you like it?'

'Yes. It feels like silk.' She continued to run her fingers over it.

'It is silk, the very best silk from the orient. I would like you to wear it for the painting. I think it will fit nicely. There's a changing room over there.' Alfonso indicated an area partitioned off by a Chinese lacquered screen. Rachel was a little taken aback by his tone, essentially ordering her to wear the gown. Surely he could have asked if she minded, or been a bit more polite. But she decided to comply with his wishes and did not dwell on it further. After all, she was being handsomely remunerated, and allowance must be made for the artistic temperament...

She took the gown off of the rack and made her way behind the screen. After she had checked that Alfonso could not see her through any gaps in the folding screen, she stripped off her clothes and put on the gown. It fitted perfectly. She stepped from behind the screen and gave a quick twirl.

'What do you think?'

'Bella, bella!' said Alfonso, smiling.

'Where would you like me to stand?'

'Come over here, and sit on this chair. I want to start by capturing your face. Look straight at me. Good, now hold that pose.' Rachael did exactly as instructed. He picked up a pencil and started to sketch on the canvas, but had not got very far when Rachael's phone rang.

'Sorry. That must be my friends checking up on me.'

'Stay still, don't move. I'll answer it for you.' Alfonso picked up the phone from the table by the door where Rachael had placed it when she had entered the studio, and answered.

'Pronto. This is Alfonso de Bartolo. Would you like to speak to Rachael?'

'Bongiorno, Mr Alfonso. Yes, please, is she there?, asked Simon.

'Stay in pose, Rachael! I will bring the phone to you.' He did so and Rachael held it to her ear.

'Hi, it's Simon. I'm just checking you're ok.'

'I'm fine, Simon. We're just getting started.'

'Are you sure?'

'Yes! Totally. Anyway, I have to go as Mr Alfonso is impatient to continue. Chat later. Bye!' Alfonso clicked the phone off and replaced it on the table by the door.

'Sorry about that, but I did ask them to call.'

'No need to apologise, Rachael. Now move your head slightly to the right. That's it! Try and stay as still as possible.' Rachael watched Alfonso as he continued to sketch her from behind the canvas, entranced by his blue eyes focusing intently on her. After a while she felt self-conscious staring back into his eyes and decided to focus instead on the coat rack behind him.

Presently he picked up his palette and squeezed tubes of paint of different colours onto it, before applying the paint to the canvas with a selection of brushes.

Rachael was lost in her thoughts until they were interrupted by Isabella entering the studio. She looked somewhat distraught.

'What is it, Signorina Isabella?' asked Alfonso.

'It's my mother, Signor Alfonso. She's had a bad fall. She's in the hospital - I'm afraid I must go and see her.'

'Of course. Don't worry, I can look after the Gallery.'

Isabella quickly gathered her things and left. Rachael was surprised that Alfonso seemed to show little concern for Isabella's plight. He just continued painting.

'Oh, poor Isabella. I hope her mother is ok,' said Rachael.

'Her mother does it all the time. She always bounces back. Sometimes I think she does it deliberately to get her daughter's attention. She says Isabella does not visit her often enough.'

'I see.' Rachael thought it was a rather drastic way of seeing her daughter.

'Well now. I think we will stop here for a break and go for some lunch. Are you hungry? asked Alfonso.

'Yes, I'm starving.'

'Good! Then I'll phone my housekeeper and have her prepare something. We can be there in twenty minutes.'

'Be where?'

'Castello Bartolo, of course. If that is fine with you?'

'What about the restaurant next... ' Rachael did not finish her sentence.

'My housekeeper is an excellent cook, and I am sure you would like to see my castle. You were so interested in the painting of it.' Alfonso looked into her eyes, waiting for an answer.

'Yes...yes, of course. That would be nice.... let me just change out of this gown.'

'Come as you are, as long as you are comfortable wearing it. I can drive us there in my car.' Rachael thought for a few seconds then laughed.

'Yes, why not! I'd better let my friends know where I am first.'

'Please go ahead, while I tidy up here.' Rachael picked up her phone and texted her friends, letting them know what her plans were - or rather what Alfonso's plans were, by which time he had taken his apron off and had picked up his car keys from the table in the Gallery. Rachael looked down at her feet. She had taken her shoes off earlier to get into the red gown, and had not replaced them. She fetched them from behind the screen and returned to the chair to put them on. Having done so she stood up and thought how silly she looked, as the shoes and gown did not match.

'Put these on.' Alfonso had noticed the inconsistency before she had, and appeared with a pair of red slip-ons with a slight heel, an exact match to the ones in the painting in the Gallery. Rachael sat on the chair again and put them on discarding her own shoes. She stood in front of a nearby full length mirror admiring her reflection and was surprised that, like the gown, the shoes were a perfect fit, and even better, comfortable to wear.

'That's better. Shall we go?'

'Lead the way, Mr Alfonso.' She picked up the hat she had arrived in and followed him out into the street, waiting as he locked up the Gallery. They walked a few paces to where an open-top vintage Alfa Romeo Spider was parked. She noticed the tourists sitting outside under the umbrellas of La Gritta restaurant turn their heads to look. A couple smiled at her and Mr Alfonso. She smiled back, feeling like a 50's movie star walking the red carpet.

Alfonso started up the car with a roar. Rachael put on her seat belt and held on to her hat, as they drove away from the piazza along a side street leading up to the main coastal road. Soon they were taking the sharp bends as the car climbed higher and higher up the coastal mountains. Rachael suddenly realised she had left her phone behind in the studio.

'My phone! I forgot my phone!' shouted Rachael above the roar of the Alfa Romeo.

'No worries. I'll send my housekeeper to pick it up for you, once we have reached the Castello. We are almost there!' Alfonso hit the accelerator as they turned a bend with an even steeper incline ahead, pushing them both back into their seats.

At the top of the hill Alfonso turned into a lay-by, where tall gates marked the entrance to the castle.

He pressed a button on the ring holding the car keys, and the double gates swung open, slowly revealing a winding gravel drive that lead up to the cliff top castle, past ornate tropical plants and trees. He parked the car at the front portico entrance and they got out.

'Wow! I am seriously impressed,' said Rachael, looking up at the imposing building.

'I can give you a guided tour after lunch, if you like.'

'Yes, I would love that. I wish I had my phone right now to take some photos to show my friends. They would be so envious.'

'Please come this way.' Alfonso led Rachael to a set of stone steps leading up to the portico, with two stone lions proudly sitting on pedestals either side. As soon as they reached the large wooden door, it creaked open slowly, and there standing at the entrance was Isabella, still dressed in her yellow suit, but with a maid's apron on top.

'Welcome to Castello Bartolo, Signorina Rachael.'

'Grazie, but... what are you doing here? I thought you went to see your mother in hospital'. Rachael looked to Alfonso in confusion, then back to Isabella.

'I did. She 's fine. Lunch is ready. This way.' Isabella's tone was very businesslike.

They followed Isabella along a long vaulted corridor leading to an arched wooden door. Isabella opened it and they stepped into a vast oak-beamed hall, with tall gothic windows through which the sea was visible. In the centre of the hall lay a long dark wooden table, surrounded by antique wooden chairs with ornate carvings. The table had been prepared for lunch with two settings of plates, glasses, and silver cutlery at opposite ends of the table. Straight out of an old film, thought Rachael.

'Please take a seat. I will serve lunch.' Isabella indicated the chair to Rachael, then left through a door half way along one side of the hall. Rachael did not sit down immediately, as she was too engrossed in looking around the hall at the antique furnishings.

'This place is amazing! The parties you could have in all this space!' Alfonso watched her closely as her gaze went around the room, and waited until she sat down before sitting down himself. Isabella reappeared, carrying two plates covered by silver domes. She placed one in front of each of them. Alfonso removed the cover, passing it to Isabella, and waited for Rachael to do likewise.

'I hope you like spinach and ricotta ravioli. One of Isabella's specialities, all homemade.'

'One of my favourites too. I love it!'

'Would you like some wine? asked Isabella.

'Just a little. I've had too much of late.'

'Red or white?' asked Isabella, holding up two decanters.

'White, please.' Isabella poured the wine into the cut crystal glass on the table and walked over to Alfonso. She poured him a good measure of red wine. Rachael noted that she did not ask him his preference. No doubt she had been his housekeeper long enough to know.

'Would there be anything else you require, Signor Alfonso? otherwise I will go and visit my mother again.'

'Yes, Isabella, Rachael left her phone in the studio. Could you please bring it here, after you have visited your mother?'

'Certainly, Signor Alfonso.'

'And anything else you think I may need.' There was silence for a few seconds and Rachael again felt a hidden message passing between them.

'Yes, Signor Alfonso.' Isabella disappeared into the kitchen and returned without her apron on, heading to the hallway leading out of the building. They heard the front door slam shut and a car start up, and the crunching of gravel.

'Mr Alfonso, can I ask you a question?'

'Please do, ask me anything.'

'How long have you lived here?'

'All my life. Castello Bartolo has been in the family for hundreds of years. My parents left it to me when they passed away.'

'Are you an only child? or do you have brothers and sisters?'

'I am the only child of my parents.'

Rachael wanted to ask him who he wanted to pass the castle on to, but resisted. Alfonso had finished eating and watched Rachael without speaking, until she had finished too.

'There is fruit and pastries too, if you like.'

'Thank you, Mr Alfonso, I am totally replete.

'Perhaps some more wine?'

'I am fine. I've had too much already, thank you. Now how about that guided tour?'

'Yes, of course. This is the main dining hall, as you can see.' Mr Alfonso got up and walked to a door on the right hand side and opened it.

'And this is the library and smoking room.' Rachael got up and followed him into a large room full of antique books behind glass bookcases and comfortable looking high-backed leather reading chairs. What she did not expect to see, and which took her totally by surprise, were the paintings on the walls. Six in total, all women, all young looking and standing in the same pose as the painting Alfonso had shown her in the Gallery. They all wore the same red gown, like the one she was wearing at that moment, and all stood by a vase of peonies on a table, holding a cocktail glass. Rachael felt a shiver run up her spine and wrapped her arms around herself.

'Are you cold, Rachael? I can find you a shawl to wear if you like.'

'No... no, I'm fine.' She stared up at the painting hanging on the wall opposite the door. The necklace around the neck of the woman looked exactly like the one she had seen in the painting in the Gallery. Rachael moved to the next painting and studied it for a few seconds before moving on to the next. All the time she was aware that Alfonso was watching her closely, to see her reaction. He noticed when she looked towards a gap on the wall.

'That space is reserved for your portrait, once I have completed it.' Rachael turned to Alfonso with a quizzical look on her face.

'What about the one in your Gallery? Surely that belongs up there.'

'The painting sitting in the Gallery is a special one. It is of Signorina Isabella when she was younger, as I think I mentioned before.'

'I don't remember you telling me that.' Now that she had been told, she could picture the resemblance.

'Did I not, Rachael?'

'You probably did. I mustn't have heard you.'

'Come this way and I will show you the terrace. A great place to have cocktails and watch the sunset.' Alfonso left the library and crossed the hall to where double doors opened out onto the outside terrace.

'Now this I could get used to!' exclaimed Rachael.

The view from the terrace was spectacular, reaching far across to the blue sea ahead, with huge white clouds on the horizon and the forested mountains to either side. She could just see the part of the coastal road where she had first caught a glimpse of the castle before arriving in Portofino. A strong breeze blew her hair in front of her face, and she had to hold it back and away from her eyes.

'It looks like a storm is coming,' said Alfonso, pointing at the clouds.

'Where do those stairs lead to?' Rachael pointed to a gap on the side of the low balustrade.

'Down to the rocks and sea. There is a small jetty there where boats can moor.' Rachael walked to the edge of the balustrade and looked over to see the stone steps curving along the cliff face, leading down to the jetty. She could see the waves crashing onto the rocks, and thought about the painting of the castle by Alfonso that he had shown her in the

Gallery. She was so mesmerised by the scene that she did not notice Alfonso move to stand by her side. She gasped; she thought she saw a body in the water - that of a young woman, stretching her arms up out of the water clasping at the rocks below, trying to pull herself up onto them. Another wave came crashing in and the image vanished. She felt her head spinning; she was going to faint. She bent over to hold onto the balustrade with both hands. She felt Alfonso's arms around her waist. Rachael turned her head; his lips were moving on his blank face, but she could not hear what he was saying. All she could hear was the roaring of the waves crashing against the rocks. She looked beyond him to see Isabella standing by the double doors to the terrace, holding up her phone. Then all went dark.

Rachael opened her eyes to see cherubs and white clouds. She pinched herself to check she wasn't dreaming, then looking around, realising that she was lying on an ornately carved four-poster bed, with a painted ceiling of a biblical heaven. The door opened and Isabella appeared, carrying a tray with what looked like some steaming tea infusion.

'Drink this. It will perk you up. Come down when you are feeling better.' Isabella spoke in a clinical tone, without sympathy. Rachael sat up. She was still wearing the red gown. She leant over and took hold of the tea, taking a sip. It tasted disgusting, so she placed it back on the tray and got up, sitting on the edge of the bed. Her head felt better, so she stood up. She looked around for her mobile and found it on the dressing table. She switched it on. She had three texts, one from each of her friends, enquiring how she was. They were received ten minutes ago. She quickly texted back, telling them all was fine, as she did not want to get them unduly worried. Then she made her way down to the library where she found Alfonso sitting in a chair, reading.

'Rachael! Welcome back to the world of the living. How are you feeling?

'Fine, thanks. It must have been the wine that made me a bit wobbly.'

'I can take you back to your hotel if you like, or are you happy to continue? I would like to get on with the painting if I can.'

'Let's continue.' Rachael was keen to earn her 5,000 Euros. She didn't tell Alfonso that she and her friends had planned to leave Portofino on the next day.

'Good! let's get started, then. Come with me.' Rachael was surprised that instead of leading her to the front of the house, he led her to the back.

'Where are we going?'

'To the studio.'

'But surely your studio is back at the Gallery in Portofino - where you left the canvas?'

'I have a studio here too. Isabella has brought the canvas here.' He opened a door leading to a glass conservatory, and there in the middle was the canvas of her that he was working on. It was the first time she had seen it from the front.

'What do you think so far?'

Alfonso put on his artist's cloak and set up his palette, paints and brushes as Rachael studied the painting.

'The face is really my face. It's incredible, Mr Alfonso.'

'Good! You approve! Now, I would like you to stand like so.' He stood in the pose he wanted Rachael to adopt, and then left the room. A minute later he came back clutching a velvet box and opened it extracting a necklace.

'I would like you to wear this.' He walked over to where Rachael was standing and carefully placed the necklace around her neck. It was the necklace in all the other paintings, glittering with diamonds and rubies. She was awestruck, but tried to act professionally and hold her pose. Once Alfonso was ready, he picked up his palette and brush and continued.

Meanwhile outside the clouds came rolling in from the sea, and it grew darker in the glass studio. The wind picked up speed and came whistling over the studio, causing some of the glass panes to rattle. All of a sudden there was a flash of lighting and a loud clap of thunder, making Rachael jump. She looked out of the windows to the sea, abandoning her pose. She saw huge black clouds and further flashes of lighting, and counted the seconds before the rumble of thunder shook the windows.

'That storm you mentioned earlier has arrived, Mr Alfonso.'

'Indeed it has. I must turn some lights on, so that I can capture what I need to finish your painting.' Alfonso walked to the door and turned on the lights, illuminating the studio just as the heavens opened and it started to rain.

'Are those special lights?' asked Rachael, looking up and squinting her eyes.

'Very well spotted. They try to replicate natural sunlight. Please let us continue.' Alfonso was keen to carry on with his painting. Rachael ignored the flashes of lighting and the booms of thunder and concentrated on holding the pose that Alfonso wanted. A few times he asked her to move slightly this way or that way as she relaxed.

A couple of hours passed, and Alfonso placed his palette and brushes on the nearby table and stood a few paces back from the canvas. He studied it for a few minutes then a large smile appeared on his face.

'I have all I need!'

'Can I move now?'

'Yes, by all means. Come here and have a look for yourself.' Rachael was relieved she did not have to hold the pose anymore, and made her way to the front of the easel. She looked hard at the painting and had to admit that the woman he had captured on the canvas was indeed her; in fact it was so lifelike that she could almost have walked into it. She noticed that everything in the painting was exactly like the others in the library; the cocktail glass in her hand, the Chinese vase holding the peonies, and of course, the red gown she was wearing with the exquisite necklace. She was speechless for several moments, and then her phone started to buzz.

'It must be my friends, said Rachael. She picked it up and answered.

'Hi Rachael, its Sarah. Are you still at the castle?'

'Yes, we've just finished.'

'Well, you'd better ... the storm ... stuck there.' Sarah's voice became indistinct as the signal weakened.

'What was that, Sarah? I only got half of what you said.'

'The storm is getting worse... back now!'

'Hello! Sarah? are you still there?' The line went dead. Rachael redialled Sarah's number but all she got was a message in Italian which she vaguely understood as 'the person you are dialling is not available. Please try again later.' She tried twice more than clicked her phone off.

'Your friends?'

'Yes, they want me to go back to the hotel. Perhaps you can drive me back as it seems the storm is going to get worse.'

They both looked up when they heard a tinkling sound coming from the roof, as if pebbles were being dropped on to it. The sound grew louder and louder. Rachael rushed to the windows and looked outside to see large hailstones falling from the sky.

'We'd better leave straight away. I'll just go and change.'

'I think it is too dangerous to leave now. You must stay here.'

'It'll be fine. Look, the hail has already stopped.' Outside, the terrace had turned white from the still frozen layer of hailstones lying on it.

'You can't leave', said Alfonso, quietly.

Rachael was somewhat taken aback. 'I have to get back to the hotel and pack - we're leaving tomorrow.'

'You will stay here. I am not finished with you yet. There is one more task I have to do.'

'What do you mean? You have all you need to complete the painting.'

Rachael's guard went up when she saw his face change. His deep blue eyes seemed to have changed in the light, no longer a pleasure to look at, but somehow menacing. He took a step towards her, and she instinctively stepped back a pace.

'You cannot leave. Now that I have painted you, you belong to me.'

'What are you talking about? Take me home this instant, or I will call the police.' She held her phone in front of her, ready to dial. Alfonso took another step towards her. There was a sudden flash of lighting, and the lights in the studio went out. There followed a loud clap of thunder. She saw Alfonso move forward in the light from her phone. She turned and grasped the handle to the double doors behind her, leading out onto the terrace. The strong wind pushed them fully open and Rachael ran outside, almost slipping on the icy surface. Alfonso followed her out.

Rachael moved backwards to the balustrade at the far end of the terrace, all the time keeping her eyes on Alfonso. She held on with one hand and tried to use her phone with the other. She was drenched in no time from the sea spray and buffeted by the wind, her long hair hanging in strands over her face. She had to use the hand holding the phone to move her hair away to see how near Alfonso was. He was almost upon her.

She moved quickly to the steps leading down to the rocks below, but stumbled, almost losing her balance. She let go of her phone and watched, horrified, as it tumbled down, smashing against the rocks and sliding into the waves. Alfonso approached and she stepped further down the staircase, gripping onto the metal railing as she did. It was icy cold. She could see a small boat tied up on the jetty below, buffeted violently by the waves. It was her only chance of escape. Even though she thought it would most certainly founder in the storm, she had to give it a go. She descended the steps rapidly, stumbling all the time but holding on tightly to the iron railing. She reached the boat and loosed the rope mooring it to the jetty. Just as she was about to scramble into the boat, she felt her gown being tugged from behind. Alfonso had caught up with her. He pulled it hard and she lost her grip on the boat, and watched in despair as the waves moved it away from the jetty and out of her reach.

Rachael was roughly pulled backwards into the arms of Alfonso. He turned her around, pinioning her arms behind her with one hand and held her throat with the other. She realised he was a very strong man, and no matter how much she struggled she could not break loose. He dragged her towards the rocks and started to squeeze her throat. She couldn't breathe; she realised she was starting to lose consciousness, but she was helpless, all the while his piercing eyes boring into hers, soulless, evil.

All of a sudden he looked down. Rachael saw a look of surprise on his face. He momentarily relaxed his grip on her arms and throat, and she gasped for air. She found the strength to bring her knee up to his groin, hard. He let go of her and she slipped from his grasp, running a few paces away from him, before slipping and collapsing on the floor.

She looked up at Alfonso, standing there, frozen to the spot. She followed his gaze and was astonished to see two hands tightly clasping his ankles. The arms were coming out of the sea, and a young woman now raised her head out of the water, her long hair blowing in the wind. She was followed by another woman, then another. Rachael later thought there had been six of them in total. They all slid out of the crashing waves, crawling over the rocks, grasping at Alfonso's legs. Two of them stood up on the rocks and held on to his jacket. Each of them wore the identical red dress, and each had a diamond and ruby necklace around her neck.

'Help! Help me, Rachael! I meant no harm to come to you!' Alfonso looked to her and pleaded, his eyes luminously blue, irresistible.

The women from the sea surrounded him and dragged him closer to the waves.

'No! No!' Alfonso screamed above the howling wind. He clawed desperately at the rocks with his hands. Rachael stood transfixed, unable to move even if she had wanted to, as the women pulled him into the sea and he disappeared under the waves. The last of the women turned and smiled sadly at her before finally vanishing below the water.

Rachael picked herself up. Dazed, she carefully made her way back up the stone stairs to the terrace and back into the castle. Through the double doors she saw her three friends enter the hall, accompanied by an inspector and two policemen.

'What took you so long? I almost died!' Rachael slipped to the floor in a faint.

When she came round she was reclining on a sofa with the concerned faces of her friends looking down at her. She reassured them she was feeling fine.

'We got your text. It was only a couple of letters, and then your phone went dead. So we immediately contacted the police. Are you sure you're all right, Rachel?' said Sarah. Rachael had started a message, but had been unable to send it before Alfonso had turned on her and she had dropped her phone into the sea. Somehow it must have been sent - perhaps when it hit a rock on the way down...

'Well, I'm still alive. I'm not complaining.'

Simon found a blanket and wrapped it around her. 'What happened?'

'It's a long story.'

Just then a police woman walked in with Signorina Isabella. She was handcuffed, but looking defiant.

'I caught her trying to escape when she saw the police cars,' said the police woman. Rachael looked at Isabella.

'Why did Mr Alfonso want to kill me, Isabella? I thought he was such a nice gentleman, who just wanted to paint me. But you knew he wasn't, didn't you? Why didn't you try to warn me? To help me? '

Isabella hesitated to answer.

'Answer the question,' said the inspector.

Isabella's eyes were ice cold. 'You need to understand, Signor Alfonso is a genius...'

'Was,' said Rachael.

'What do you mean, was? Where is he?'

Rachael hesitated, looking out to the terrace.

'What happened to Signor Alfonso, Rachael? asked the inspector.

'I'm afraid he's dead.'

'No...No! He cannot be dead!' cried Isabella.

'You were saying he was a genius. Continue, if you please,' said the inspector.

Isabella took control of herself again. 'Signor Alfonso, as I said, was a genius. When he finished a painting, the subject matter became his. He captured their souls. He painted this castle we stand in, so he obtained it.'

'But he told me it was in his family for centuries.'

'Ha! He lied to you, Signorina Rachael. But in some ways it was true. He owned it completely.'

'What about all the woman he painted?

'Once Signor Alfonso had painted them, they belonged to him. Surely you felt that? Deep down you knew you were his.'

'No. You can't own a person, and certainly not me,' said Rachael.

'Signor Alfonso could not allow any other artist to capture their image, so he had to put an end to his models. It is as simple as that. Do you not understand? No? Then you cannot appreciate the depth of his greatness.'

'That is not greatness, Isabella, it is madness,' said Rachael.

'It is a small price to pay to be immortalised by such a one as Signor Alfonso.' Isabella stared at Rachael, her eyes wide. She, too, is mad, thought Rachael.

'What did he do with them? asked the inspector.

Rachael already knew the answer before Isabella spoke.

'I watched each time,' she said proudly. 'He would lure them to the castle terrace and strangle them, before throwing their bodies into the sea below.'

'What a monster!' said Sarah.

'How did you get away from him, Rachael?' asked the inspector.

'He tried to do the same to me. I ran down to the rocks. He followed me. There was nowhere to go... then he.... he.... I think he slipped on the rocks and fell into the sea.' Rachael started to cry. Simon put his arms around her shoulders to comfort her.

'Is that how he died, Rachael?' The policeman looked at her as if he was expecting her to say something else. She glanced up at him for a brief moment.

'Yes.' She thought it best to hide the truth. Who would believe her in any case?

'Perhaps you should change out of those wet clothes. Are you well enough to come to the police station to give us a full statement? Do you have any dry clothes to wear?'

'Yes, I have my own clothes in the studio. I'll change quickly and meet you all in the hallway.' She waited until they were all out of sight before walking back out onto the terrace. In her attempt to escape from the clutches of Alfonso, she remembered that the diamond and ruby necklace had slipped off her neck. She scanned the terrace and sure enough, there it was, glinting at the top of the stairs leading down to the jetty. Rachael briskly walked over and picked it up, glancing around to make sure no one had seen her.

'This belongs to me now, I think. My payment for being a model. And a little extra for the inconvenience.' Rachael smiled to herself and tucked it away. Only then did she make her way back to change into her own clothes.

Rachael gave a full statement at the police station, keeping back only the story of the drowned women and the necklace. She was driven back to the hotel to pack for their departure the next day. The storm had passed, and they decided to have a grand farewell dinner at a local restaurant.

'Well, that should teach you to get sucked in by a psycho,' said Peter.

'You should have stuck with me,' joked Simon.

'The sad thing is, after risking your life for 5,000 Euros, you ended up with nothing.'

'Well I certainly have learnt my lesson. I'll take things a lot slower next time and not be so blinded by the way a person looks. But I did come away with a little souvenir.' Rachael opened her shoulder bag and pulled out the diamond and ruby necklace. Her friends gasped with disbelief. She grinned at them.

'Are the gems real?' asked Sarah.

'I'm sure they are. They'd better be, after what I've been through. I'll find out when I get the necklace valued before I sell it. But I have a feeling that my Student Loan, like Signor Alfonso himself, will be no more.'

THE MOSAIC OF ROME

The Chambers Dictionary defines a mosaic as, 'the fitting together in a design of small pieces of coloured marble, glass, etc.' These pieces can be regular or irregular in shape, held in place by plaster or mortar and covering a surface, such as a wall, floor or ceiling.

It was this ancient art, dating back four to five thousand years, that interested Neil. His speciality, in particular, was Roman mosaics. A harmless, innocent art form, so he always thought. But let me tell you how Neil discovered that it could have an unexpectedly dangerous side.

Neil had decided the best way he could pursue his interest in Roman mosaics was to enrol in a workshop in his favourite Italian city, Rome. The four week course was quite expensive, as it included not only the tutoring, but all the materials and tools that he could possibly need. It also included visits to the museums and archaeological sites of Rome. Neil had booked a small apartment near to the mosaic studio and workshop, located a short distance from the Coliseum.

The first morning was spent learning mosaic making techniques. The students were introduced to the different types of materials, and learnt how to cut them into the shapes they required using specific tools for the purpose. Goggles were issued for health and safety reasons to protect their eyes from flying chips of marble or glass. In the afternoon, they were shown various mosaic designs and images so that they could think about what they wanted to create.

Unlike the majority of the other students in the class, Neil understood the principles of mosaic making and already had some practical experience of making simple designs. However, he decided that rather than making geometric shapes with the pieces of marble and glass, which he thought was easy, he would be more adventurous, and make a mosaic of a face or figure.

The next day the course teacher organised a visit to several museums and archaeology sites around Rome to give the students further ideas for their particular mosaics. Everyone, including Neil, took photos of the designs and images that interested them, as they listened to their teacher giving them further information about what they were looking at.

It was in the National Roman Museum that Neil found the mosaic that was the greatest interest to him; a head of Dionysus, the god of wine, as a boy. It was very colourful, and showed the youth wearing a crown made of grapes surrounded by a border, consisting of a single wavy line of white marble filled in either side by black, red, blue and yellow marble pieces.

'May I have your attention, everyone. The museum closes in 10 minutes. I hope you have decided on the subject matter for your Mosaic. I will see you all tomorrow at the workshop, and we will start to create our mosaics!' said the teacher. Everyone clapped, then slowly made their way to the exit of the museum.

Neil was the last to leave, as on his way out he had stopped in front of another mosaic; that of a charioteer standing with his horse. He stared at the face of the charioteer, drawn in by his piercing hypnotic eyes, and was oblivious to the passing of time until the lights flashed to indicate that the museum was closing.

'Please make your way to the exit, sir,' said a nearby voice. Neil turned his head and saw a curator holding the gallery door open for him.

'Just one second, please,' said Neil. He quickly turned his phone camera on, and took a snap of the mosaic. He turned and started to walk towards the curator, then paused as a shiver ran up his spine. He sensed that someone behind was watching him.

'Thank you for visiting,' said the curator, and closed the doors to the mosaic gallery. Neil left the museum and walked back to his apartment, all the time thinking about the mosaic of the Charioteer, with his piercing eyes. He couldn't work out why the image had affected him so much.

After having a rest and freshening up, Neil decided to go to a local bar for a drink, one the teacher had recommended for making the best Negronis in Rome. A few of the other students were already there, and he joined them, forgetting all about the mosaic of the Charioteer. He followed this with dinner at a nearby restaurant that served excellent homemade pasta, and washed it down with a few glasses of wine. By the time Neil got to his apartment it was well gone midnight. He was not too concerned, as the mosaic classes started at ten every day, quite a reasonable time.

Sleep came easily with the help of the Negroni and wine, but he was restless for most of the night. Images of the Charioteer invaded his dreams. At one point, he was riding a chariot drawn by four horses as it raced around the Circus Maximus in ancient Rome, to the roaring of the crowds of spectators. This disappeared to be replaced by the face of the Charioteer in the distance, surrounded by utter darkness, coming towards him, getting bigger and bigger each second, his piercing eyes boring into him all the time until it was only inches away. Neil awoke from the nightmare sweating and panting, struggling to catch his breath. He switched his bedside lamp on and decided to read for a while. An hour later he was asleep again.

The next day he started working in earnest on creating his mosaic. He got into a routine of working on his piece from ten in the morning to five in the afternoon, only stopping for lunch. In the evenings, most of the class continued to meet up for Negronis and dinner, during which they discussed each other's progress, as well as a host of other topics. The class was quite cosmopolitan, with students from all over Europe. Neil was the only person from the U.K.

Two weeks into the course, Neil was setting the last pieces of marble he had cut to create the head of

Dionysus. All that was left to do was the border, and then finally the grouting, to complete the mosaic. Neil decided he needed another photograph, as the one he had taken on his first visit to the museum had been accidently deleted. The copy he had printed out and enlarged had become ruined after he had spilt a mug of coffee over it, so he set aside a few hours to revisit the National Museum.

He remembered exactly where the original mosaic had been located, and made his way there. On entering the gallery, he immediately spotted the mosaic of the Charioteer. As he walked slowly past it he again felt a chill run up his spine. He was convinced the piercing eyes of the charioteer were following his progress to the nearby Dionysus Mosaic so dropped his eyes to the horse instead, but looked away when the horse's eyes also seemed to follow him.

Neil convinced himself that the creator of the mosaic had intended the eyes to follow you, something so many great artists seemed able to achieve. He dismissed it from his mind, and concentrated on what he had come to see, the Dionysus Mosaic. He called up a photo on his phone that showed the progress of his mosaic, and compared it to the original in front of him. Reassured that his work was a close match to the original, he clicked a few shots of it before heading to the gallery exit. He stopped when the lights flashed a few times, and glanced at the time displayed on his phone. It read shortly before three; surely too early for closing time.

He turned and looked around the gallery. It was empty, with not even a guard in sight. When Neil turned back, he was facing the mosaic of the Charioteer. He stared at it. Surely there was something different about it, compared to a few minutes before, when he had come in. What was it? He moved closer, as the lights in the gallery had dimmed a little. He noticed that the Charioteer was smiling in a way that gave him the creeps; an evil looking smile. He was drawn closer, then all of a sudden the room went dark; pitch black.

Neil tried to find his phone and switch on the torch, but could not feel it in his pocket. Had he dropped it? He tried to move, but felt paralysed. At that moment the gallery lights came back on, and the sight that Neil saw shocked him to the core.

He wanted to scream but couldn't; he was looking at a mirror image of himself, standing in the gallery and looking directly back at himself. But there was something about the image that was not him - this version of him was giving an evil smile and staring back with piercing eyes.

'No! No...this can't be..... what is happening?'

'Yes, I like this body. It has been such a long time since I was last able to do this.'

'Do what? Who are you?' asked Neil, realising that communication seemed somehow to be occurring with no actual speech or sound.

'I am the Charioteer. Every so often I get a bit bored, and like to leave the mosaic and live a little. Last time was ...oh, let me see... I think there was a war on...which one I couldn't tell you. Then before that, someone had found me under the ground, and I took over their body for a short while before returning. Now I must go and experience the world again, and see how it has changed.' The Charioteer gave Neil a chilling grin, and looked towards the exit, where a group of tourists had just arrived on a tour.

'No, no! You can't leave me here!' Neil shouted, but no one could hear him.

'There's no need to worry. I'll be back soon.'

'When?'

'Seven days. That is the time I am allowed. I was created in seven days, and I've never been able to leave for longer. I keep hoping, but so far... Well, maybe one day...'

'Come back! Come back!' Neil watched in despair as his body, now containing the Charioteer, strolled past the group of tourists and left.

The group of tourists stood in a semi-circle in front of him. A woman carrying a stick with a Chinese flag on it started to give a lecture. The tourists pointed their phones and cameras at him and snapped away. All Neil could do was to watch and hope for his body to return. He remembered the Charioteer's final words: 'Well, maybe one day...'

THE BEAST OF GIBRALTAR

Clifford pulled the curtains aside and opened the sliding door to the balcony. Taking in a deep breath, he smiled and glanced at the sun as it emerged from the sea to the east; a golden orb that became brighter by the second, lighting up the scattering of low-lying clouds. The salty sea air instantly energised him as he emptied his lungs and took in another deep breath. Looking to the west he spotted the Rock of Gibraltar coming into view on the horizon, shrouded by a layer of mist with only the peak visible, illuminated by the rays of light from the rising sun.

He felt a soft hand on his shoulder and turned to give Gabriella a kiss on the lips followed by a deep hug. They had recently got married and were on their honeymoon, passengers on the Crystal Excelsior cruise liner on a ten day tour of the Mediterranean. Their last port of call was to be Gibraltar before heading back to Southampton.

'Look at that magnificent view,' said Clifford. He held onto Gabriella's waist with one hand as he pointed to the Rock of Gibraltar with the other.

'I always wanted to visit that place but never managed to get there, even though I was born in nearby Marbella,' said Gabriella.

'Well, now you will be able to visit the place where I was born!' Clifford turned to her again and gave her another kiss.

'From this distance it looks like a mountain slowly emerging from the sea as we get closer.'

'Maybe it's the fabled City of Atlantis, reappearing.'

'Yes! Atlantis! How romantic!'

'Waiting for the arrival of their new King and Queen!'

'You mean us?' said Gabriella, mocking him innocently.

'Of course, darling! They giggled and hugged each other closer.

Soon the magnificent Rock of Gibraltar was looming ahead of them. They noticed the liner cut its cruising speed and start to decelerate. This was followed by an announcement on the intercom from the captain, informing the passengers that they would soon be docking in the port. Clifford and Gabriella enjoyed the view as the liner travelled around to the west side of the Rock, where the docks were located, and slowly pulled into their allocated quayside spot.

'We'd better get dressed and have a quick breakfast before we go sightseeing, as we're only here for half a day. I wouldn't want you to miss anything, Gabriella.'

'I'll be ready faster than you think.'

'Really?' said Clifford, mocking her. She cocked her head sideways and gave him a forced smile before disappearing into the bathroom.

She reappeared fifteen minutes later allowing Clifford to take his turn. Half an hour later he reappeared.

'What took you so long? I've been ready for hours!'

'Ha, ha, quelle humeur!'

'We Spanish say "Que gracioso eres" '

'Give me ten minutes to put some clothes on and I will be ready to rock and roll!'

Twenty minutes later they made their way down to breakfast, then they left the ship to catch the shuttle bus which would take them to the start of the cable car leading up to the top of the Rock of Gibraltar.

'I hope you're not scared of heights.'

'You should know me by now, Clifford. I love heights!'

Clifford bought their tickets just as a cable car approached and having waited for the passengers to disembark, they stepped in along with a few other passengers from the ship. The door slid shut and the cable car started its ascent up the rock. Most of the passengers faced outwards enjoying the spectacular views of the port area out of the glass windows.

'Look! There's our ship,' said Clifford, pointing at the docks.

'It looks like a toy ship from here,' said Gabriella. No one in the cable car was talking apart from them. They were too busy clicking their cameras and taking photographs and videos with their phones. It did not take long before they arrived at the cable car top station. As soon as the doors opened and they all stepped outside, a strong breeze almost blew their hats off and everyone had to reach to hold them down with their hands.

'I almost lost my hat there,' said Gabriella as she held onto it with one hand and brushed her long dark hair away from her face.

'That's not the only thing you have to watch out for up here!' said Clifford.

'Yes, I already know. The locals call them "monos"!' said Gabriella. She was referring to the Barbary macaques, the only wild monkey population living on the European continent.

'I just want to remind you that no matter how cute you may think they are, they can get pretty aggressive and bite you if you annoy them.'

'My friends from Spain who have been here said watch out for your belongings, especially your sunglasses and bags, as they will snatch them and run off.'

'They're well known for that. In fact once when I was playing up here as a teenager with some friends we saw a group of elderly tourists from one of the cruise liners. One of the ladies was busy taking photographs of two baby apes sitting on a wall, when suddenly an adult approached and snatched her wig off her head, leaving her completely bald. We couldn't stop laughing.'

'Oh, poor woman. That wasn't very nice of you. I hope she had a spare one back in her cabin on the ship.'

'I hope so too, otherwise she would have to spend the rest of her holiday bald,' said Clifford giggling.

'It's not funny, Clifford! Poor woman,' said Gabriella. Clifford did his best to suppress the giggling.

'Let me take you to the monkey feeding station first. It's only a short walk away. That's the best place to see them, then we can go and visit St.Michael's Cave, and if we have time, wander around the series of tunnels carved by the military to defend the Rock. But before all that let's look at the view from here.'

They went to the railings of the viewing platform, which provided an uninterrupted 360 degree view. Looking north was the steep mountain peak of the Rock of Gibraltar, on either side of which the Spanish coastline curved away as far as the eye could see. To the east, looking down the mountainside, could be seen the tourist beaches of "Sandy Bay" and "Catalan

Bay", and to the south, the Mediterranean Sea with the coast of Africa just visible.

'Does it make you weak in the knees looking down?' asked Clifford.

'Not really. As I said, I love heights. Let's go to the monkey feeding station now. I'm keen to see them. Are they monkeys, or apes?'

'They're actually monkeys, but everyone calls them "The Apes", so I suppose it's a matter of preference.'

He led the way along a cliff edge path to the feeding station, where several monkeys - or apes - were waiting on the walls. 'Stand in front of those ones. I want to get a photo of you with them,' said Clifford. Gabriella instinctively held tightly onto her hand bag, and took off her hat, holding it with the same hand. She used the other to hold her sunglasses. She was taking no chances.

'Shall I stand here?' She stood a few feet away from the wall.

'No, go closer to the wall.' Gabriella turned to look at the apes, who were showing no interest in her presence, just staring sideways. She looked to see what had caught their attention. It was other tourists further along the wall.

'That's perfect. Now stay still and smile.' Gabriella felt somewhat uneasy being so close to the apes, but managed to produce a genuine smile as Clifford lined up his mobile phone and took a few shots. Gabriella was startled when a young girl screamed as a baby ape leapt onto her. She turned to where the sound had come from and watched as the girl's parents took photographs of the baby ape sitting calmly on her shoulder. A few seconds distraction was all it took for Gabriella to be yanked backwards against the wall. She saw Clifford run towards her, almost in slow motion. She felt a pain on her throat as the necklace she was wearing snapped away from her neck. She turned quickly to see the apes scampering rapidly along the wall, one of them clutching her necklace.

'Are you all right darling?' Clifford had reached her and had wrapped his arms around her.

'Those bloody monkeys stole my necklace!' She was about to give chase, but they disappeared over the edge of a set of steps leading down to the Ape Den below.

'Are you hurt, Gabriella?'

'No, I'm fine. Did you see that? I just blinked and they stole my necklace.'

'Yes, I did. I told you to be on your guard. They can move really fast.'

'We'd better go down to the Ape Den and see if we can retrieve it.'

'I think you have to be realistic... I don't think you'll see that necklace again, darling. I'll buy you another one before we get back on the ship. We can go shopping.'

'Fine, but let's go down all the same.' They made their way down several stone steps until they reached an area where a large number of apes sat observing the tourists or grooming each other. Gabriella scanned the scene on the off-chance that she would spot the ape clutching her necklace.

'They all look the same,' she said, before giving up all hope.

'They probably think the same about us. Let's go and have a look at St. Michael's Cave. I've heard it's quite spectacular. Gabriella breathed out a sigh of defeat and took hold of Clifford's hand as he led her south towards the cave. He paid the entrance fee and collected a pamphlet explaining the history and features of the cave, and read extracts from it to Gabriella as they entered.

'It says here that that the caves were well known to the ancient Greeks, Romans and Phoenicians, and evidence of occupation by prehistoric humans has been found.'

'Wow! Look at the size of this cave,' said Gabriella glancing up at the numerous stalactites hanging down from the cave ceiling.

'This is called the Cathedral Cave, and is the largest of the chambers, currently used as an auditorium for concerts and "son et lumiere" shows.' Clifford continued to read from the pamphlet. They followed the marked route deeper into the cave, noticing how the stalactites and stalagmites were colourfully lit. Clifford stopped reading out aloud when he noticed Gabriella was already reading one of the many displays giving information about the cave several paces ahead of him, and walked over to join her.

'It says here that during the Victorian era, archaeologists found prehistoric artefacts such as stone axes, arrow heads and shell jewellery,' said Gabriella. She brought her hands up to her neck, thinking about her stolen necklace.

'Look here, Gabriella darling. It also says that officers who served here during times of conflict passed their time during quiet periods by exploring the many passages within the cave system. Some got lost never to be seen again, so stay close to me and don't go wondering off.'

'Don't worry. I won't go wondering off.' Gabriella took hold of Clifford's arm to reassure him, even though she knew he was only teasing her. She let go after a few seconds and walked over to the next display panel, leaving Clifford to finish reading the one he was standing in front of.

As Gabriella read this panel, a tour guide passed behind her followed by a small group of visitors. She listened as the tour guide told his excited group that they were in for a magical surprise soon, that only their exclusive group were allowed access to. Gabriella was intrigued and decided to follow them.

They passed through a series of descending chambers. She hesitated at one point, glancing back to see if she could still see Clifford in the hope that she could get him to join her, but he was now out of sight. She decided to continue to follow the group, which had now stopped at the entrance to another chamber. A thick metal chain ran across it, with a 'no entrance' sign attached to the middle. The guide unhooked the chain and held it to one side, allowing his group to pass through one by one, then reattached it to the wall. Gabriella approached the chain, then glanced back to make sure she was not being watched, before unhooking it. She walked into the entrance of the passageway, attaching the chain back to the wall.

Gabriella walked along the narrow passageway and heard the gasping sounds of the visitors echoing in the chamber ahead. She quickened her pace without making a sound and discreetly poked her head around to see into the chamber. There before her stood the group with their backs to her, looking at an underground lake of crystal clear water. The lights installed in the lake produced a serious of dancing patterns on the roof of the chamber as water dripped onto the surface.

The group, along with Gabriella, were mesmerised by the magical atmosphere for a few minutes. It was broken eventually by the guide suggesting they should get ready to leave. Gabriella quickly turned and headed for the exit, making it out just before the group entered the passageway. In her haste not to be seen she turned into another passageway to her right, which also had a 'no entrance' sign across it, and ducked underneath the chain. She waited for the group to pass, listening until their excited voices dwindled, then ducked back underneath the chain to see the last of the group turn the corner ahead. As they did the movement sensor lights dimmed in all the passageways and chambers.

An eerie silence descended around her with only the distant sound of dripping water coming from the chamber with the underground lake. Gabriella paused when she heard a scraping noise coming from behind her, from the passageway she had been hiding in. She held her breath and listened. There it was again. The sound of something scurrying along, too loud to be a rat, she thought. Gabriella took out her mobile phone from the small bag she held around her shoulder and switched on the torch. She shone it into the passageway, moving it from side to side. She gasped aloud when two eyes shone back at her, and she stepped a few paces backwards. The eyes blinked a few times and grew bigger as whatever it was approached her. Her instinct was to turn and run, but she hesitated when she saw something else glinting in the dark, something she recognised.

An ape appeared in clear view, clutching a necklace in one hand - her stolen necklace. Gabriella moved closer, then lifted the chain across the passageway, letting it drop to the floor. The ape turned and ran up the passageway into the darkness.

'That's mine!' shouted Gabriella, giving chase. The passageway turned left and right, then down, descending deeper and deeper. Eventually she arrived in a chamber full of massive stalactites and stalagmites, some of which had fused together to form pillars of rock. She shone her mobile left to right, and there, peering at her through a window between two pillars, was the ape. Neither of them moved for a while. Gabriella noticed how warm the cave was; she had expected it to be cold and damp. The standoff continued for several more minutes, each of the participants waiting for the other to make a move.

'That's my necklace. Give it back to me!' she repeated. The ape continued to stare at her from the safety of the pillars.

A cool breeze from the right made Gabriella turn her head. She thought she saw a figure moving across the room. It came to a standstill a few feet away from the ape hiding behind the rock pillars. Gabriella moved her torch to illuminate the figure, and was astounded when she saw a man dressed in the same manner as some of the photographs she had seen earlier on the display panels. He was staring directly at her. He looked like a Victorian archaeologist. Without uttering a word, he extended his arm out to the ape, with his palm out. Gabriella followed the outstretched arm with her eyes to where the ape had been hiding behind the pillars. But now, instead of seeing the ape, she saw only its shadow against the wall behind. The shadow started to grow, becoming upright and taller until it filled the height of the back wall of the cave. A hairy hand appeared from behind the pillar, holding her necklace and moving towards the Victorian archaeologist. She brought her hand to her mouth to stop herself from screaming as a hairy creature, almost human in form, came into full view and handed the necklace to the archaeologist.

'I believe this belongs to you,' he said - the first words he had uttered since appearing out of nowhere. The creature turned its head to look at Gabriella and growled, showing off its fang like teeth.

'Don't be frightened. She's quite harmless, really,' said the archaeologist. He held out the necklace. Despite his reassurance, Gabriella approached the man cautiously. Once she was in front of him, she held her palm out. He let go of the necklace and it dropped into her grasp. The creature made a low growling noise again, prompting the archaeologist to turn and address her.

'Don't fret my dear; I'll get you a nice shell necklace that will suit you better than that metal one.'

'Thank you.' It was all that Gabriella could say as she stepped backwards, keeping her eyes and torch on the archaeologist and the beast. All of a sudden her torch flickered. She looked down at it and saw that the battery was very low. She looked back up; momentarily glimpsing the shadow of two apes against the back wall of the chamber, before the light of her torch flickered once more and died, sending the chamber into total darkness. She listened to hear any sound in the silence, but did not hear anything. They must have gone.

Gabriella felt her way back along the walls of the passageway until see saw some light coming from the chamber ahead. She exited from the passageway, making sure that the chain was pulled across and secured. Before she headed back towards the Cathedral chamber she put on her necklace, and on entering immediately spotted Clifford.

'Where have you been? I was so worried you had got lost. I was about to alert the staff here.' He wrapped his arms around her.

'I wasn't lost. I followed a private group to the most amazing underground lake.'

'You should have let me know where you were going.'

'Yes, I'm sorry. I didn't have time.'

'What's this? You found your necklace! Where? Clifford stood back to have a better view.

'In there,' said Gabriella pointing into the chamber.

'But how? I thought after that ape had snatched it, we would never see it again.'

'Well, it seems she brought it in here, and I was able to retrieve it.'

'That's absolutely incredible.'

'Yes, I know!'

'We ought to be getting back to our cruise ship. It leaves in an hour.' Clifford glanced at his watch. 'At least I don't have to buy you another one now!' He smiled. 'Or maybe I should anyway'.

'We'd better go. But I might remind you of that at our next port of call'.

'By the way, how did you know the ape was female? We only got a quick glimpse of its back as it as ran off with your necklace.'

'You won't believe me when I tell you. It's best I save the details for when we are back on the ship and you have a strong cocktail in your hand, darling!'

THE WATERS OF CAPRI

I heard a distant sound, familiar but elusive. The longer I listened, the louder it grew, a constant, regular beeping sound. I tried to open my eyes but my eyelids seemed to have stuck together. I tried again, and slowly my eyelids parted. I saw a fuzzy figure walk past a window, through which the sunlight was pouring in. I blinked a few times to clear my vision, and was surprised to see the figure of a nurse standing over me, checking something attached to my arm. She smiled. Behind her stood a young man, also smiling down at me. The beeping sound continued at regular intervals coming from my left hand side. I turned my head slightly and saw mechanical equipment; hospital equipment.

'How are you feeling?' asked the nurse. She checked the thing attached to my arm. I realised it was a drip, attached to a plastic sack above me containing some liquid.

'Tired,' I said.

'It's good to have you back,' said the man. I did not recognise him.

'How did I get here?' I asked.

'It's best we let her rest,' said the nurse to the man. He nodded, and then bent down to give me a kiss on the forehead before leaving. The nurse also left, closing the door behind her. I had no recollection of how I had ended up in hospital, and the more I tried to remember, the more my thoughts became muddled.

I must have fallen asleep, for I awoke when an orderly came into the room wheeling a trolley. He was followed by the nurse, who went to the side of my bed and pressed a button, causing the back of the bed to rise up, allowing me to get to a sitting position. The orderly moved a hospital table in front of me and placed a plate of food on it.

'It's your favourite!' he said enthusiastically. I looked down at the plate and saw a piece of salmon with roast potatoes and peas. Since when had salmon been my favourite meal?

'I'm sorry, but I can't eat this,' I said. The orderly looked at me, confused.

'But you've had this every Monday for the last few weeks. Your husband told us it was your favourite food.' He looked at the nurse, then shook his head, wheeling the trolley away again but leaving the plate.

'My husband?' I said, looking up at the nurse. She was busy rearranging and puffing up the pillows behind me to make sure I was comfortable. She looked at me sympathetically.

'Yes, the man who was here earlier is your husband. His name is Daniel, Francesca. You must be patient. All your memories will come back in time.'

'Francesca? That isn't my name. My name is....' But I couldn't remember what my name was. 'My memories? What happened?' I asked the nurse.

'There is no need for you to get stressed, Francesca. The doctor will come and see you later. He'll explain everything to you. Now please eat, and you will feel better for it.'

What was the nurse talking about? I couldn't remember an accident, and I certainly couldn't remember ever getting married! When did all this happen? I looked down at the food, and as I was hungry, I ate the potatoes and peas, but I left the salmon. Soon the orderly came back and took the plate away. The nurse reappeared with several pills on a tray and a glass of water.

'It's time to take your medication, and then I suggest you get some rest,' she said.

I didn't want to rest. I wanted answers, but I had too many questions going through my mind. I still couldn't remember the accident, and importantly where and how it had happened. As the nurse said, I would have to wait until the doctor came to see me later. She pressed a button and the top half of the bed lowered down. She made sure I was comfortable, then adjusted the window blinds to cut out some of the sunlight streaming into the room, and left.

I drifted to a place where I was neither awake nor sleeping. I was lying on my front, feeling the heat of the sun on my back as I stared at the surface of the blue sea, the sun sparkling off the surface. I was on a yacht, anchored in a small cove, bobbing up and down on the gentle waves, not thinking of anything in particular. All of a sudden I heard a whisper coming from far away, a word that I could not fathom out. I listened, but all I could hear was the lapping of the waves on the side of the yacht. Then I heard it again, much louder this time; it sounded like "where?" I held my breath and listened intently for a few seconds, but all I could hear were sea birds calling. It must have been those that I had heard, so I emptied my mind of all thoughts and rolled onto my back, facing the sun.

No sooner had I settled down when I heard the anguished sound of a woman's voice. 'Where am I?' she said. I opened my eyes and sat up; looking around the yacht, but there was no one in sight. 'Where am I?' she said again. 'Hello, who are you? Where are you?' I called out, scanning the waters around the yacht.

'Help me, I am lost,' the woman said.

'How can I help you? I can't see where you are.'

'Help me, please! Help me!' the voice now shouted. I awoke from the dream I must have been having and looked around the empty hospital room. I listened out for voices but only heard the noise of the functioning hospital equipment. The familiar nurse entered the room and checked the reading on the machines, as she must have been remotely alerted to the fact that my heart beat was racing. As soon as she was satisfied that it was back to normal she left the room.

I stared at the white wall opposite, where the sunlight filtering through the blinds was creating patterns on the wall like the sunlight reflecting off the surface of the sea. I was mesmerised for I don't know how long, when it happened again. It started with a voice in the distance, as if in a tunnel, and grew louder by the minute. This time I was fully awake, and I again asked the same questions. Then I realised what I was doing. I was talking out loud to an imaginary voice in my head. It all stopped when the door opened, and in walked a doctor.

'Good afternoon,' she said.

'Good afternoon Doctor. Are you new?' I did not recognise her.

'I'm Doctor Montessori. I've been dealing with you since you were admitted, a few weeks ago.'

'What happened to me, doctor? How did I get here?' She did not answer immediately, but instead picked up the board at the end of the bed and checked what was on it.

'You were involved in an accident off of the coast of the island of Capri, and brought here to Naples State hospital.'

'What kind of accident?'

'You were swimming in the sea by some rocks when a freak wave dashed you against them. You friend Elena saw it happen, and dived into the water to save you. A local fisherman also saw the whole event unfolding, and before your friend could reach you, he pulled you out of the water. You were unconscious. A helicopter brought you here to this hospital. You were in a coma for the first two weeks.'

'I can't remember anything of what you have just said.'

'No need to worry, your memories will come back in time. You have to be patient. You had quite a knock to your head.'

'But doctor...' I was about to tell her about the voices in my head but I stopped. I rubbed my head.

'Are you in pain, Francesca? I can prescribe some painkillers if you are still experiencing those severe headaches.'

'No, I'm fine it's just that... I'm starting to hear voices in my head. And my dreams are getting very strange. I dream I am on a yacht...then a voice keeps asking questions.'

'There's no need to worry. That's quite normal. It's your memories starting to come back to you. Your subconscious mind is reconnecting with your conscious mind. In addition, the drugs that we have been giving you can also cause some confusion. As I said before, it will all settle down in time. You just need to be patient, Francesca.'

'Why does everyone insist on calling me Francesca? I'm sure it's not my name... yet what is my name? I can't remember...' I looked up at the doctor, not really expecting a response. All she did was give me a sympathetic smile. She wrote something on the medical board. Just then the door opened, and in walked the nurse. At least I did remember her.

'You have a visitor,' she said, and stood aside as the man, the one whom I had seen before and who had claimed to be my husband, entered the room carrying a bunch of flowers. He came forward and kissed me on the forehead, handing me the flowers.

'Hello Francesca. You're looking much better. Isn't she doctor?' he said.

'Yes, she's making great progress. Now I must go, as I have other patients to attend to,' said the doctor, and departed.

'Let me take those flowers and put them in a vase for you.' said the nurse, and promptly left the room as well.

'Thank you for the flowers. The nurse told me your name is Daniel. Sorry, but I don't recognise you. I am told I'm suffering from memory loss.

'Yes, my name is Daniel.'

'And you're my husband?'

'Yes, I am indeed that lucky man.' He looked down at me. It was difficult to read his expression. Was it pity, that I could not remember who he was?

'How long... how long have we been married?' I asked cautiously.

'Not long at all. As newlyweds, we've spent our honeymoon in Italy, travelling around. We decided to stay another week on Capri with friends who have a place there...' He stopped talking and brought his clenched fist to his mouth. I could see tears welling up in his eyes.

'Carry on... tell me what happened, Daniel.'

'Two days into our stay with them, they - they being Lorenzo and Mia, in case you can't remember - suggested we spent a day on their yacht. We were joined by your friend Elena. It was the most perfect day to go out, with a gentle breeze and calm seas. We had moored by a cove, and while I, Lorenzo and Mia were preparing lunch on board, you decided to go for a swim, leaving Elena sunbathing on deck. When we were ready to eat, we could not see either of you anywhere. We panicked, worried you both might have got into trouble or drowned. Then we saw the fisherman in his boat moving towards the yacht, with you lying limply on board. He said he had found you by some rocks with a gash to your head, and had pulled you out of the water. Thank goodness you were still alive, and we immediately called the authorities who brought you to this hospital. I'm afraid...' Daniel did not finish his sentence as I gasped with a sudden bolt of pain. I held my head.

'Elena! Elena! It's me, Francesca,' said the voice in my head.

'Francesca, are you all right? Are you in pain?' Daniel was clearly shaken. Images started to appear before my eyes. I could see myself in a register office; I was wearing a wedding dress and next to me was Daniel. He smiled as he placed a ring on my finger. I heard someone say you are husband and wife... people started to cheer... then the scene shot to a yacht floating on the blue sea. I saw my friend sunbathing on deck, and told her I was going for a swim to cool off before lunch. I dived into the water and swam towards some rocks. The sea was rough by the rocks, then all of a sudden a huge wave engulfed me and all went dark.

I looked up. Daniel's lips were moving but I couldn't hear him. He looked worried. He stood and left the room and quickly came back with Doctor Montessori. All I could hear were the words 'Elena, Elena, it's me, Francesca...' repeated over and over again in my head. I must have passed out. When I woke up, Daniel was sitting by my bedside.

'Francesca's awake, Doctor,' he said. The doctor came over and shone a light into each of my eyes in turn. She gave a reassuring smile and said that I was fine. I looked directly at Daniel.

'Daniel, could you do something for me?' I asked.

'Yes, anything you want, my darling wife, anything.'

'Can you bring me a mirror?' It had just occurred to me that in all this time I had been in hospital, not once had I seen my own face. I had relied on the staff to look after me.

'Yes, of course, I'll ask the nurse.'

Soon the nurse came back with a small circular mirror and handed it to me. I raised it to my face, not sure what to expect. I was relieved when I remembered who I was. The face in the mirror was me, Elena. I turned to the man sitting by my bedside and now recognised him. He was indeed Daniel.

'I now know who I am,' I said.

Daniel, the nurse and Doctor Montessori all looked on in silence. I turned back to stare at my face in the mirror, and gasped as the image dissolved into a blur. A few seconds later the image sharpened again, and I saw the face of Francesca! I felt my heart stop, and saw the doctor and nurse looking towards the monitors. I turned too and saw that the heart monitor was flat lining. It all happened in slow motion... I felt my vision blurring and my mind melting. I saw the face of Francesca... She was crying and saying 'Goodbye, my dear friend Elena.'

'Goodbye, Francesca,' said the voice in my head. The words were repeated over and over, becoming quieter each time until they ceased altogether. I turned to face my husband.

'Where is my friend Elena? You never mentioned what happened to Elena?' Daniel put his arms around me and hugged me tightly as tears appeared in my eyes.

THE BLACK ROSE OF BARCELONA

All streets have a history, be they new or hundreds of years old. People may ask how a new street can have a history, when it has just been built. Those people might be correct if the street and its accompanying buildings are constructed over virgin soil. However, in most cities, new tends to be built over the old; sometimes over and over again, so much so that the previous happenings in the street are not just distant history, but the forgotten past. The lives of the occupants and the events affecting their lives are all but gone...or are they? Let me tell you about my experience of a typical Spanish city street I resided in during my stay in Barcelona, while writing my first novel.

I had started to write with enthusiasm from my one-bedroom flat in central London, but that enthusiasm dwindled as the weeks passed by. The weather was miserable and it had not stopped raining for weeks on end. My ideas had dried up; to the point I got writer's block. I thought that was only experienced by successful and well known authors, not someone writing their first novel. In the end I decided to leave London and head to warmer climates to inspire me to complete my writing project, a tale of life in a street spanning several generations. I had started my writing based on the history of life in a typical London Street, but realised it was not, how shall I say, exotic enough. In addition the market was flooded with books on the subject.

I choose the city of Barcelona, and rented a flat for six months in a street called 'Carrer de l'Arc de Sant Ramon del Call'. The owners were very keen to rent the flat to me, and I was amazed at finding such a central location on my limited budget. I spent the first days familiarising myself with the neighbourhood, and found a nice coffee shop where I could have breakfast each morning and a small local supermarket that sold all I could possibly need as regards provisions. In those first few days I also visited some of the tourist sites; Sagrada Familia cathedral, Gaudi's Casa Mila and The National Catalan Museum of Visual Art among many others.

On the fifth day I started writing in earnest. Having changed locations, I edited much of what I had already written about the life of a fictional family over several generations, changing the names from English to Spanish. By the end of the first week I had decided to scrap all that I had written and start afresh, to take into account the different customs and way of living of the Catalan people.

Before writing a single word, I would start each morning with a visit to the coffee house nearby. Soon they got used to me and started asking about what I was doing in Barcelona. I did my best to communicate in my schoolboy Spanish, and somehow we kept a sort of conversation going. After coffee I would go back up to the apartment and write for several hours, stopping briefly for a light lunch of bread, cheese and various hams. I resisted going to restaurants for lunch as I would be tempted to have a glass of wine or two, resulting in very little writing being accomplished in the afternoon.

One evening, after a successful day of writing, I decided to dine out at a local restaurant, nothing too pricey. I found one called 'La Rosa Negra', that on the outside looked a little rundown, but inside was a traditional Spanish taverna. I ordered half a litre of red wine and some tapas, as was the custom in these places. I tended to dine early for Spain, so the place was empty when I arrived. Soon it filled up with locals, all of whom were greeted by the owner as if they were long lost friends. The diners were all of a certain age. They dressed in rather traditional, somewhat dated clothing. The women wore long elegant dresses under their fur coats, and the men were suited with long smart coats, hats and silk scarves. Rather overdressed, I thought, for an ordinary restaurant.

Each of them acknowledged my presence as they passed the table at which I was sitting with a smile and a 'Bona nit,' which I should have been pleased with, but their dark eyes gave a different message that made me feel somewhat uneasy. I reciprocated the greetings.

By the time I had finished dining, the restaurant was full and the atmosphere was jolly, as one would have expected. I wanted to stay longer and order another carafe of wine, but decided against it as there was much work to be done the next day and I wanted a clear head. I called for the bill. It arrived promptly, and satisfied it was all correct I fished in my wallet for euro notes to pay. As I did, the restaurant door opened and a tall distinguished looking man entered, sporting a long pointed beard and wearing thin framed round eyeglasses, as worn by scholars, I thought. Immediately the restaurant became silent, all attention turned to the new arrival. The men stood up as he surveyed the restaurant diners. The owner greeted him profusely and took his coat, hat and scarf, handing them to an assistant. He then escorted the man to a table at the back of the restaurant. As he passed amongst the diners, each one moved a hand to their left breast as if pointing out something and nodded their heads once. It was then that I noticed each person was wearing a brooch, the same type of brooch, a black rose. My first thought was that the man must be the local Spanish mafia boss who came to the restaurant to dine after a hard day of, well, doing what mafia people did.

The man arrived by my table, and I noticed he too was wearing a black rose brooch. He momentarily stopped and stared at me. I saw his eyes noticing I was not wearing any brooch. I gave him a weak smile and said 'Bona nit.' He blinked once and turning to the owner said, 'The man's wine glass is empty,' then proceeded to his table. As soon as he sat down, all the men sat too and the restaurant erupted into chatter and laughter again. Soon a waiter appeared with a glass of red wine and placed it in front of me.

'You'd better add the wine to my bill,' I said.

'It's ok, this is on the house,' he said, looking over to the table at the back.

As soon as I had finished the wine I left the amount of the bill on the table plus a tip, and then got up to leave. I turned to look at the man at the table at the back and noticed that the table was now empty. I assumed that he had gone behind the velvet curtains at the back of the restaurant, as in the short time it took me to drink the extra glass of wine he had not walked past me. No doubt he was conducting mafia business with the owner.

Back in the apartment I sat and read for a while, but could not concentrate as my mind kept drifting back to the restaurant. I decided my dining experience there, and my encountering the other diners, in particular the mafia boss, would feature in my novel. I grabbed my notebook and pen, and jotted down a few ideas and plot lines. I noted down that everyone in the restaurant wore a black rose brooch. What was that all about? Perhaps they were all part of a dining club and met once a week...The Black Rose Dining Club. That's what I should call it in my novel. I turned on my iPad and used the internet to do a search on the subject. I typed in 'La Rosa Negra,' but nothing came up. I tried 'Black Rose of Barcelona' and scanned the pages that came up -

various tattoo parlours and images of Black rose tattoos, but nothing about a dining club. After a while I yawned and decided it was time for bed. I would ask the owner of the coffee shop tomorrow, and perhaps at the restaurant too, and see if they could give me further information.

It did not take me long to fall into a deep sleep, helped by the red wine I had consumed. I awoke suddenly when I thought I had heard a scream coming from below the apartment, and checked my phone to find out what time it was. The display gave the time as 2.30am. I heard a bubbling noise, then a loud hiss, as if a steam engine had arrived into a station. The hiss sound dwindled to silence until all I could hear was the occasional creaking of the ceiling timbers. The central heating radiators in the apartment and in the whole building were quite ancient, and I was still not used to the strange noises it would make in the middle of the night.

I was drifting back to sleep when I heard the smashing of glass and a shriek coming from outside. I immediately switched the bedside lamp on and went over to look out of the window. Two cats were fighting, and had knocked an empty wine bottle that had been left on a small metal table outside the wine bar opposite. It had smashed to the pavement stones. I rapped on the window and both cats stopped fighting and momentarily looked up at me, before one of them chased the other further down the street.

I went back to bed and switched out the bedside light, but sleep eluded me. My mind kept wandering back to the restaurant, and images of black roses appeared in my vision even though my eyes were closed. I must have dozed off, as when I awoke again, light was streaming through the slats of the wooden blinds that I had forgotten to adjust when I had viewed the fighting cats.

The street outside was already bustling with the sound of delivery trucks and vans on route to supplying the local restaurants and stores with produce. I could also hear a group of men outside the local coffee house chatting as they had a quick coffee before commencing their tasks for the day.

I joined them, but sat inside, as even though the sun was shining it was still a little chilly for this time of morning.

'How are you this morning Senyor Writer?' asked Mateo, the proprietor, a rotund man with red rosy cheeks. I had told him my name several times, but he always called me Senyor Writer.

'I am fine, Mateo. Ready for whatever the day brings!' I said.

'Your usual?

'Yes, thank you.' Soon a coffee arrived and a croissant de almendra.

'Mateo, I know you're busy, but can I ask you a question?'

'Sure, go ahead,' he said, and listened as he continued to serve customers.

'I went to a restaurant last night and everyone was wearing a black rose brooch. What does it mean?' Mateo did not answer but I saw that his face became serious. He handed over a coffee that he had just made to the customer waiting, who glanced over at me before finding a nearby table to sit at.

'Mateo?' He looked up from the counter he was now wiping with a cloth.

'The black rose. What does it mean?' I repeated.

'I do not know.' His reply was abrupt.

'Who can I ask?

'I don't know. I cannot talk now. I am busy, customers are waiting to order.' Mateo's mood had changed within the space of a few seconds. He took the orders of the few customers who were there then disappeared into the kitchens. I finished my breakfast and left the necessary euros on the table. I imagined the restaurant would be closed this time of morning, so made my way up to the apartment with the intention of paying a visit at lunchtime to the restaurant, not to eat, but to enquire about the black rose.

The morning's work was very fruitful, and I became so engrossed in writing that I only briefly stopped for lunch in the apartment before continuing well into the afternoon. I did not want to interrupt my chain of thought, so I decided to leave visiting the restaurant to the evening. I stopped writing when I noticed the street light outside switch on and stretched my arms upwards, yawning at the same time. The time display on my iPad read 6pm. Good! It was time to crack open a bottle of wine and have a glass before heading out to the restaurant.

I decided to dress up a little and instead of wearing jeans and a jumper as I had done the previous night, I changed into a pair of black slacks, a shirt and a smart jacket as I had noticed that all the diners last night were very well dressed. Come to think of it, I did feel as if I was in a film set when the place was full, as a lot of the diners wore vintage clothing.

I finished my glass of wine and headed out walking the short distance to the restaurant. On arriving I stood staring at the place. Was I too early as a metal shutter had been pulled down covering the entrance and windows on which graffiti had been sprayed. I glanced at my mobile phone which displayed the time as 8pm. Surely the place should have been open by now. What day was it? I thought as some restaurants are closed on a specific day to give the staff a rest day. It was Saturday! The busiest day of the week as far as restaurants were concerned. It should be open.

I walked further along the street until I found another restaurant that seemed to offer the same kind of cuisine and at a price I could afford and dined there instead. It was full of trendy young people and again I felt somewhat out of place in my smart attire as they were all in jeans and casual tops. I asked my waiter when I came to pay the bill if he knew why the 'La Rosa Negra' restaurant was closed tonight but he said that he was new to the area and did not know of it.

I exited the restaurant and made my way back to the apartment. As I approached La Rosa Negra, I noticed someone standing in front of the metal shutters dressed all in black. It looked like a woman but she was dressed in a peculiar outfit perhaps she was on her way or had come from a fancy dress party. Maybe she also thought the restaurant was open this evening and was surprised it was not. She seemed to be holding something in her hand as I got closer, so I slowed down my pace almost to a standstill. I saw her bend down to place it on the floor in front of where the entrance was, albeit behind the metal shutter. It was too dark for me to see what it was as her body blocked the street lighting casting a shadow across the entrance. I continued to watch as she stood up straight, turned and started to walk at a pace away from me just as the street lights flickered on and off. I momentarily looked up at the nearest one and when I looked back down the street she was gone.

I turned my attention back to the object she had left and walked to stand over it. I was astonished to see a single black rose lying on the floor. I bent down to pick it up and have a closer look but held back, in case the woman came back and accused me of trying to steal it. There was a gust of wind and it stated to rain, so I did not linger further and walked at a pace to my apartment a few doors up.

That night the same thing happened, I heard a bubbling noise and the hissing sound of steam escaping but this time it was coming from below. I got out of bed and lay my ear against the floor. It was coming from the apartment below but how could it be as there was no door to the space below as you entered the building. Perhaps access was via the building next door. There was a thump and the sound ceased. I listened for a few more seconds then decided it was probably the natural sounds of these old buildings and got back into bed.

No sooner had I settled down when I heard a scream. Not those cats fighting again, I thought to myself and this time I stayed in bed. I am sure after a few more days I would get use to all the noises of the building and neighbourhood and not think twice about it.

The next morning I awoke as usual and left the apartment descending the stone stairs to the front door looking forward to my first cup of coffee of the day. I stepped out onto the street and stopped in my tracks when I noticed a black rose lying on the ground. I glanced left and right to see who had left it there then bent down to pick it up. I was just about to bring it up to my nose and smell it as I was intrigued by the possible aroma a black rose would have, when I heard someone shouting. I turned to see Mateo racing towards me.

'Stop! Don't smell the rose! He shouted. Before I knew what was happening he reached out and snatched the rose from my hand and threw it into the street. A passing car ran over it flattening it completely.

'What did you do that for?' I asked a little shocked by his actions. He could not answer immediately as he was bent over holding his knees and trying to get his breath back. When he did eventually stand I saw his face was red.

'Sorry, I am not used to being this energetic in the mornings.' No doubt he had run from the coffee house to snatch the rose from my hand.

'You did not answer my question, Mateo.'

'Let's go and have some coffee and I will explain.' We made our way to the cafe and sat at a table outside. Mateo signalled to his assistant who subsequently brought out two cups of coffee.

'So?' I waited until he had taken a sip of his coffee.

'That rose was poisoned.'

'Poisoned? What do you mean?'

'The rose was laced with a lethal poison, a single sniff and you would have died on the spot.'

'But who would want to poison me? I haven't done anything. I have just arrived in this city.'

'Let me explain. It's to do with where you are staying.'

'The air B & B apartment you mean?'

'Yes. It has a history and not a good one at that.' He took another sip of his coffee.

'Carry on.'

'The building was owned by a famous alchemist in the 14th century. He had his workshop on the ground floor where he spent his time doing what alchemists do. Above the workshop the family had apartments where they lived, one of which is where you are staying now. People who have stayed there complained of strange noises in the middle of the night. In fact most moved out after a short stay.'

'Are you telling me the place is haunted? That would explain all the funny hissing and bubbling noises I have been hearing coming from the room below. I thought it was the plumbing and radiators in the building.'

'Well let me continue with the history of the place.'

'Go ahead. I'm all ears.' Mateo looked at me confused.

'All ears?'

'An old English expression meaning continue I am listening.'

'Anyway, the alchemist had a daughter who met a young man and wanted to marry him. She pleaded with him to ask permission from her father, but he knew the father would not give it as he was from an unknown family. She ended the relationship and found another lover instantly. He was so angered by her rejection that he decided if he could not marry her, no one else would. He would poison her. He visited the alchemist, her father and acquired a poisoned rose that could kill with a single sniff. One night he called up to her room and convinced her that he still wanted to marry her and would get her father's consent. He threw up the deadly rose and she was felled after taking in the lethal scent. Her father found her dead and realising it was the rose he had poisoned himself, put a curse on the house.'

'So was it the daughter, or her ghost that tried to poison me?

'Neither. It was the spirit of the Alchemist. He tries to poison anyone who stays in the apartment on the anniversary when she was herself poisoned.'

'Is that anniversary today by any chance?'

'Yes today,' said Mateo.

'Well thank you for saving me, I owe you my life.'

'That's ok. I do it every year, whoever the occupant of the apartment is. Now I must get on before all my customers start to arrive.'

'Oh, one more question Mateo. The other night I had dinner at that restaurant down the road, you know, La Rosa Negra. I tried to dine again there last night but it was closed. Any idea when it opens again.' He looked at me with a confused look on his face.

'La Rosa Negra has been closed since the 1940's. Are you sure you got the name correct. Maybe you drank to much wine,' said Mateo laughing.

'Yes it was definitely called that. It was full of customers and what was odd, I thought was that they were all wearing a black Rose broach. I assumed it was a private dining group.'

' I am told they are victims who also stayed in the alchemist's house and all posioned by a black rose. Before I took over the running of this coffee house, it was run by my uncle. He too looked out and warned the occupants of the house on the anniversary date of the tragic death of the alchemist's daughter, however there were several years when neither me nor my uncle were here,' said Mateo as if in a trance. I concluded that they too made an appearance once a year.

THE GIRL FROM TANGIERS

At last, we had arrived at the port of Algeciras after our month long grand tour of Spain. At Madrid Airport we had hired a car and first headed north to visit Bilbao, then south east to Zaragoza followed by Barcelona, staying a few nights in each city. Thereafter we tracked the Mediterranean coast to Valencia, Cartagena and all the way down to Malaga, then inland to Granada, Cordoba and Seville. We decided to take in Cadiz before heading to Algeciras to drop the car off and take a bus to Gibraltar to catch our flight back to the United Kingdom.

'Matt, I'm not sure if I want to go back home just yet. I'm having such a great time,' said Olivia, as they walked the short distance from the Rent-A-Car drop off point to the airport bus stop.

'Me neither,' said Matt.

'Autumn term doesn't start for another three weeks. I know you wanted to get back early and get things organised, but why not stay for a little while longer?' Both Matt and Olivia were studying for their respective degree courses at Oxford University, about to embark on their final year.

'Sounds a great idea. What did you have in mind?' Matt was also having a wonderful time travelling and did not want it to come to an end.

'I checked the internet on my phone, and there is a ferry service from the port to Ceuta in Morocco. We could hire a car and go to Tangier. I read it's a most amazing city to visit. We could even drive to the Atlas Mountains for a few days and also stay in Fez before returning to Tangier.'

'Wow! You certainly have done your research,' said Matt surprised. Usually it was Matt who would organise their travel plans. Olivia left him to the task as he was so good at it.

'Well what do you think? Olivia asked as they arrived at the bus stop and joined the short queue of other travellers going to the airport.

'I've never visited Morocco. I'm up for an adventure, but first we'll need to rearrange our flight from Gibraltar.'

'I've checked that too, and it won't cost too much to change the date of our return flight.'

'Let's do it then!' said Matt.

He took out his credit card and mobile phone and started to amend their booking to two weeks hence. As he did this the bus arrived, and all the waiting passengers boarded with their luggage, except Matt and Olivia. The driver told them in Spanish that this was the bus to the airport and urged them to board, but Olivia informed him that they were going to the ferry port not the airport. He looked at her in confusion and pointed to his right before shrugging his shoulders. He closed the bus doors before moving away.

'Right, that's all done. I've amended our return date and it only cost 30 euros each.'

'Brilliant, let's go then. There's a ferry leaving in two hours.'

They left the bus stop and walked back to the ferry port, passing the car drop-off point, and went into the ticket office where Matt purchased two return tickets to Ceuta. They then headed to the ferry terminal coffee shop to await the departure of the ferry.

Soon they were on their way, admiring the view of the magnificent Rock of Gibraltar as they sailed south to Ceuta. The journey took only an hour and thirty minutes and they were off the ferry and through customs within twenty minutes. They headed to a nearby car rental dealer, and immediately hit a snag. When they enquired about car hire, from the middle aged man sitting behind a glass partition, he informed them in his limited English that all their available cars had already been rented out. Apparently it was the start of a three day public holiday.

'Is there a bus we can take to Tangier today?' asked Matt.

'No bus. Bus gone,' he said.

'Can you tell me what time the next bus is?'

'Mercredi,' he said.

'That's Wednesday, in case you didn't know,' said Olivia. As well as Arabic, a lot of Moroccans also spoke French, a language that Olivia had learnt at school.

'But today is Thursday. That's almost a week away! What are we going to do?' said Matt. He was tempted to blame Olivia and tell her that she should have let him do all the travel arrangements, but wisely decided against it.

'What about the train?' asked Olivia in French.

'No train today. Train go next week.'

'Then we're stuck here for a week,' said Matt feeling totally defeated.

'Maybe I can help you,' came a voice from behind. They both turned to see another man sitting in one of the chairs by the window. They had not noticed him when they had come into the car hire office.

'I see that you need a car to get you to Tangier', he said. His English was good.

'Yes we do, but as you heard there are no more cars left for hire, and the last bus and train for a week have gone,' said Olivia.

'You can use my car. It's just outside.'

'That's very kind of you, sir, but don't you need to use it yourself?' asked Matt.

'It's ok, I don't use it much. In any case my brother can drive me anywhere I need to go.'

'Your brother? Where is he?'

'Behind you. He owns this place. I just came in to see how he was.' They both turned and looked back at the man behind the partition and saw the resemblance to the man sitting down.

'Are you sure about this? We'll need it for two weeks' said Matt.

'I am sure,' he said looking up to his brother who nodded in approval.

'Ok. How much is it per day?'

'There is no charge. All you have to pay is the insurance and make sure it has a full tank of petrol on your return.'

'That's extremely generous of you. We must give you some money for the hire.'

'No money. I insist! Now, my brother will do the necessary paperwork and then you can be on your way.' It only took a few minutes for him to fill in the form and hand a copy to Matt, once he had paid for the insurance, which seemed surprisingly a small amount.

'Have a nice journey to Tangier,' said the man behind the partition.

'Come with me,' said his brother. Matt and Olivia followed him out of the office to the back of the building where a white Renault 4 was parked. They both stared at the car, speechless. The car was rather dilapidated with dents all over. It was certainly old, as indicated by the number plate 100- 40. The number 40 was the registration for the district of Tangier and 100 the number of cars registered.

'It's a classic made in the 1970's. I bought it a few years ago and have been meaning to restore and repaint it, but never mind, it still goes!' They continued to stare at the car, still lost as to what to say to the man. He handed the keys to Matt and showed him how to switch the engine on, in case he didn't know. He explained all the unique features that they couldn't find in modern cars.

'Are you sure about this? Is it safe to drive?' Olivia whispered to Matt.

'Yes, it's safe to drive,' the man said, having heard her. Olivia smiled at him as he went to open the boot so that they could put their small suitcases in. Once this had been done, Matt sat in the driver's seat and Olivia in the front passenger seat. Soon they were waving at the man as they drove out of the port area.

'Now I know why he didn't want to charge us anything for the car,' said Olivia.

'And the insurance was so low. Well at least it runs!' said Matt, and they both laughed out loud. They left Ceuta and joined the N16 road that wound its way along the northern coast towards Tangier. One hour into the journey Olivia looked down at the radio on the simple dashboard.

'I wonder if this radio still works?' She turned the dial and heard a click, then moved it slowly clockwise. The radio crackled for a while, then they heard what sounded like a human voice.

'See if you can get a better reception.' Matt briefly took his eyes off the road and glanced down at the radio. Olivia eased the dial slightly clockwise and anti-clockwise until the voice became clearer.

'It sounds like the word "Bonjour".'

The sound deteriorated to a crackling again, then the whole radio went silent. Olivia turned the dial on and off several times, then gave up, saying that it was dead.

They were both surprised when without being touched the radio came on, and the crystal clear voice of a young girl uttered the word 'Bonjour'. Matt and Olivia looked at each other then down to the radio, when the words were repeated a few seconds later.

'Bonjour.' The radio went silent again. They listened intently then jumped when the radio crackled and the same word was repeated over and over again becoming faster and louder each second until it was just a wall of sound. Then suddenly the radio cut out, leaving them in silence. Matt slowed the car down as they were turning around a sharp bend in the hill they were ascending, when Olivia screamed out.

'Look out Matt!'

He swerved the car and slammed the breaks on, coming to a stop by a siding. Luckily there was no one behind them or any oncoming traffic, as otherwise there would have been an accident for sure. They got out of the car, shaken, and looked back where a few metres behind the car stood a girl of about seven or eight years old, by the look of her.

'Oh my God! I almost ran her over. What was she doing in the middle of the road?' said Matt. He looked around to see if there were any other cars parked in the vicinity, but there weren't. Olivia approached the girl and squatted down in front of her.

'Bonjour, ça va? Es-tu blessé?' she said, then repeated the words in English for Matt's benefit. 'Are you all right? Are you hurt?' The girl shook her head and clutched a rag doll with long black hair in her hand. They noticed that she was smartly dressed, even if a bit old fashioned.

'Are you lost?' asked Olivia in French. The girl shook her head from side to side.

'Ask her where her parents are,' said Matt. Olivia did so, and the girl pointed in the direction they were travelling.

'Tangiers?' Matt asked. She nodded her head up and down. Matt and Olivia looked at each other, rather perplexed by how the girl had got there.

'Do you want us to take you to your parents in Tangiers?' asked Olivia.

The girl did not answer; instead she walked to the car and waited.

'I think we can take that as a yes,' said Matt.

Olivia opened the car door for her and she climbed in.

They joined the girl in the car and continued their journey. On the way, Olivia managed to coerce out of the girl her name, which was Aziza, and where her parents lived. It happened to be in the old city, quite near to where they were going to stay. Every few minutes Matt glanced in the mirror to make sure Aziza was all right. All she did was to stroke the hair of her doll as she looked out of the window at the passing scenery.

It was not too long before they entered the city. At a large roundabout they joined the 'Avenue Mohammed VI', the main road leading along a stretch of sandy beach, up to the port area. They parked the car just outside the old city quarter. Inside, most of the streets were too narrow for cars. Matt gasped when, having put the handbrake on, he glanced in the mirror to an empty back seat.

'Where did Aziza go?' They turned around in case she was crouched on the floor, but she was not there. Turning around again Olivia spotted her crossing the main road heading towards the old city.

'There she is!' Olivia pointed through the windscreen.

'How did she get out of the car so fast without us seeing or hearing her?' asked Matt.

'I have no idea, but we'd better follow her and make sure she gets to her parents' house, safely.' Olivia got out of the car and headed in the same direction as Aziza.

'Hang on! What about the luggage?'

'We'll come back for that. Just make sure the car is locked.' Matt locked the car and ran to catch up with Olivia. They saw Aziza turn down a narrow street and followed her. She then disappeared left into an even narrower passageway, then through an arch into a small square with a fountain surrounded by buildings. Olivia called out to the girl but she ignored her, entering a similar passageway through an arch on the other side of the square. They continued to follow, hot on her tracks, and started to run to catch up with her. They emerged from the darkened passagway into a circular paved area surrounded by four or five storey dwellings.

'Where did she go?' said Matt puffing to catch his breath. They scanned the area but there was no sight of Aziza.

'Look, there's her doll on the floor by that house.' They walked up to a large ornate wooden door in front of which lay the discarded doll. Olivia bent down and picked it up.

'This must be her parents' house. She must be inside.'

Matt pulled down a string attached to a several cowbells and the sound alerted the occupants that someone was at the door.

'That's odd,' said Olivia, looking down at the doll.

'What's odd?'

Before Olivia had a chance to answer they heard footsteps on a stone floor inside, and the door opened. A middle aged woman wearing a head scarf appeared and gave them a wary look. She assumed they were tourists asking for directions, having got lost in the labyrinthine streets of the city.

'I think this belongs to your daughter,' said Olivia, handing over the doll.

'We found her wandering the road outside of the city and drove her back to Tangiers. We have no idea how she got there. We followed her here to this house, said Matt.'

The woman took the doll and stared at it for a while, then turned to call back to someone. Soon a wrinkled old woman appeared supporting herself with a walking stick. She too stared at the doll.

'It belongs to Aziza,' said Olivia.

'Aziza?' said the middle aged woman, somewhat confused.

'Yes she is your daughter. Isn't she? Olivia realised that the woman was probably too old to be her mother. Perhaps she was Aziza's grandmother. Then who was the elderly lady with the walking stick? The elderly lady spoke to them in English.

'You'd better come inside.' Matt and Olivia followed the women in and were shown into a large room off of the stone hallway. The room was furnished with white leather sofas, ornate tables and gold painted lamps, with oriental carpets on the floor.

'Please sit. Bring some tea for our visitors would you, Latifah? They look thirsty,' said the elderly woman.

'Yes mother,' said Latifah and disappeared.

'What are you names?'

'I'm Matt, and this is my girlfriend Olivia.'

'Olivia...that is a nice name.'

'What is your name?'

'Nahla.'

'That's a nice name too,' said Olivia, and was lost for what to say next.

She started to feel somewhat awkward with all the pleasantries, especially as Nahla was observing them quite intently without speaking. Matt and Olivia gave each other a reassuring smile. Their eyes wandered around the room, looking at all the paintings and furnishings. They were relieved when Latifah came back carrying a tray with small glass cups of tea and a plate containing Moroccan sweets. She handed a cup to each of them and offered the sweets. Both took one and thanked her.

'Where is Aziza? Asked Olivia. The two women looked at each other.

'Tell them, mother,' said Latifah. Nahla looked down at the glass of tea she was holding and was silent for a while as if in a trance. She then spoke without looking up.

'When I married my dear husband, who is no longer with us, we spent our honeymoon in Paris. We loved all things French, unlike our parents, who hated the French. When we came back and settled in Tangiers we wanted to be reminded of the wonderful time we had had in Paris, and one day, to my surprise, my husband arrived home and said he had something for me. He took my hand and led me out of the ancient city to the car park by the port, where he showed me what the surprise was. It was a car - a French car, a Renault 4, that had just arrived in Morocco. I was delighted, and we were the envy of all our friends. A year later I became pregnant and gave birth to twins. As soon as they were old enough to travel, we took our twins everywhere; on picnics to the wonderful beaches in the country, across the deserts, and up to the Atlas Mountains. We were so happy during those years. Then suddenly it all ended.' Nahla started to cry and took out a silk embroidered handkerchief to wipe away her tears.

'What happened, Nahla,' asked Olivia softly.

'Continue, mother,' said Latifah.

'One day we were coming back from a picnic. It was a glorious sunny day. The twins were playing in the back of the car when, as we approached a bend in the road, an oncoming lorry lost control. My husband swerved the car to avoid a head on collision with the lorry but it clipped the back of the car, and we went into a spin. One of my girls tried to hold onto the side of the door, accidently opening the door... I cannot continue. Latifah, you finish the story.' Nahla started to sob into her handkerchief and Latifah stood by her side comforting her.

'When the car finally stopped spinning, I looked around and my twin sister Aziza was gone. She had fallen out of the car. Just before the accident she had taken her seat belt off to pick up her doll that she had dropped onto the floor of the car. Had she kept it on, she would be alive and here today. My mother, father and I were uninjured but when we got out of the car, Aziza was nowhere to be found. She must have fallen over and into the steep ravine below the road. The police and rescue searched and searched for days but they never found Aziza's body.'

'That is so tragic. I'm so sorry for your both,' said Olivia.

'Thank you for finding Latifah's doll. She must have fallen out of the window when she was cleaning the room upstairs. The doll normally sits just inside on the window, ' said Nahla.

'I like to air that room and always open the window when I clean it. The room was the childhood bedroom I shared with Aziza,' said Latifah.

'But, I thought the doll we found outside was Aziza's,' said Olivia.

'We both had the same doll, except mine had brown hair and Aziza's one had black hair.'

'I knew there was something odd when I picked up the doll outside. It wasn't Aziza's. It was Latifah's!' Matt and Olivia noticed a confused look appear on her face. They looked at each other, lost for what to say next.

'May I wash my hands? they are a bit sticky from eating the delicious sweets,' said Olivia.

'Mine too. I'll come with you,' said Matt. Latifah showed them where they could wash their hands and left them to it.

'Matt, we know that we found Aziza by the roadside, right? We gave her a lift to Tangiers and followed her to this house. We didn't imagine it all, did we?' whispered Olivia.

'We definitely didn't imagine it.' Matt picked up the towel from the rail by the sink and started to dry his hands, and then handed it over to Olivia.

'Are you thinking what I'm thinking?'

'That Aziza is a ghost?

'Yes, exactly, but how do we tell her family that? asked Olivia.

'I think it's best we keep that to ourselves. We don't want to upset them further.'

'Don't you think they should know?

'That Aziza is a ghost? I don't think that is a good idea and in any case they wouldn't believe us. I'm not sure I believe it myself now. Shall we go back in?

'We'd better, before they get suspicious. It's about time we left anyway.'

'Would you like some more tea? Asked Nahla.

'That's very kind of you, but we must be getting on. We left our luggage in the car.' Nahla and Latifah thanked them again for finding the doll and saw them out into the square. Just before they departed, Matt asked them a question.

'Nahla, out of curiosity, what colour was the car that your husband drove?'

'It was white. I remember the number plates to this day, as it was one of the first to arrive from France. 100-40. Why do you ask?'

'Nothing really. I was just curious.'

As Matt and Olivia bid Nahla and Latifah farewell, they noticed the look of confusion on both their faces. They turned and started to walk away from the house, and heard the door close behind them. For no apparent reason they stopped walking and turned around to look at the house one final time. They both gasped when they spotted Aziza gazing at them out of the top floor window. She waved at them and smiled, clutching a rag doll in her hand.

'Aziza is home now,' said Olivia.

'Indeed she is,' said Matt. They both smiled and waved back to her before disappearing into the darkened passageway leading back the way they had come.

THE MARSEILLE GHOST TOUR

'Hello, let me introduce myself. My name is Jules, and I will be your guide tonight on the famous ghost tour of Marseille.'

Richard, Melanie and Harry listened intently to every word Jules said and took notes. Unlike the other ten tourists in the group, they had booked the tour for a particular reason. They were all undergraduates studying for a degree in English and Creative Writing at York University, and had chosen Ghost and Horror stories as the subject matter for their final year projects. Every time they visited a city they would join the local ghost tour to gather material for their own stories. The intention was to write ten short stories each, and collect them together into a book that they could publish.

They had already visited London, Paris, Madrid and Rome, and had built up sufficient material, but decided to include Marseille as Melanie's parents owned a three bedroom apartment in the old harbour area, which they could use during their Easter holidays. Melanie's mother was French, born in Marseilles, and owned the apartment with Melanie's English father.

'The first place we will visit is the House of La Dame Blanche - the White Lady. Follow me, please,' said Jules.

'Not another White Lady story. Every town or city seems to have one,' said Richard.

'Yes, she certainly gets around,' said Melanie, giggling.

'I thought a White Lady was a cocktail,' said Harry. 'Much more fun.'

'Ha, ha, not funny, Harry.'

They followed Jules and the group to a tall old house, the ground floor of which had been converted into an upmarket cafe.

'This house was owned by a rich trader in the 19th century, who married a woman much younger than himself. As soon as they were married, the trader's character changed for the worse and he wanted his wife to stay at home all the time and start a family.

She had different ideas, however. She wanted to go out with her friends, stay out late and party. So the rich trader locked her in a room in the attic. One day, she tried to escape out of that small window up there by tying several bedsheets together...'

'Let me guess. She slipped and fell to her death,' said Richard.

'And now walks the premises as a ghost,' said Melanie.

'And, of course, she was dressed all in white when she died,' added Harry making them all snigger. Jules had stopped talking.

'Please come closer to the group, the three people at the back, so that you can hear me better,' said Jules. He knew that they were mocking the story he was telling the group. Everyone turned around to look at them and they moved a few paces forward, feeling a little guilty.

'Come on guys, be serious,' whispered Melanie from the side of her mouth.

'As I was saying, the young wife tied the sheets together then lowered herself down from the window, but she lost her grip and fell to her death. People have reported seeing a lady dressed in a long white gown climbing down from the window late at night, then falling and disappearing before she reaches the ground.' Several of the tourists in the group gasped.

'Probably reported by a few drunken people coming from the harbour bars,' said Richard. Melanie elbowed him in the stomach before he could say another word.

'Please take photos, if you wish, and then we will go to the next place on our itinerary.' Jules watched patiently as the group snapped away with their phones or professional looking cameras.

The next place they stopped at was a butcher shop, where several grisly murders had taken place. Jules explained that there was a local Mafia connection, but before he had a chance to outline the story, the three of them had already guessed the theme.

'I bet the sausages the butcher sold were tasty,' said Richard.

'I bet they were...special,' said Harry grimacing.

'Yuk!' said Melanie, then followed with: 'Gruesomely fascinating, though!'

By the time they had visited the eighth location it was a quarter to midnight, and the three of them were feeling tired and somewhat bored. Each ghost story was so clichéd that they had already heard the same story several times before.

'So much for inspiring us. Same old stories,' said Richard.

'Yes, they are a bit,' said Melanie.

'Well, there's one more to go. Let's hope this one inspires us, and maybe even scares us,' said Harry, not really expecting much.

'Here we are, back at the old port, where I will tell you the last story on this ghost tour. It was here, amongst these old warehouses, where it happened. As you can see, today a lot of the warehouses have been tastefully converted into art galleries, restaurants and cafes, but there was a time when you would have been risking your life to come here. For hundreds of years, traders would arrive here in their ships, carrying goods to trade. As the people of Europe became wealthier the demand for goods increased, especially for exotic items from far off lands. These warehouse were used to store those goods before they were transported to all the regions of France and beyond to the big cities of Europe.'

For the first time that evening, Richard, Melanie and Harry were interested by what Jules was telling them. Perhaps this was going to be a story they had not heard before.

'It was the year 1854. A sailing ship arrived from the French Congo in Africa, carrying all sorts of goods to trade, including a very special cargo destined for the newly opened Zoo in Marseille. The Zoo proprietor had heard rumours of an exotic animal that frequented the waters of the Congo River deep in the African jungle, and had offered a vast sum of money if it could be caught and brought to Marseille. The proprietor thought that if he could display the creature in his Zoo, it would be the event of the century, and people would come flocking from all parts of Europe to see it, making him a fortune. However, as the crate containing the creature was being unloaded, the crane cable snapped and it dropped into the water. When the crate was recovered subsequently, it had smashed open and the creature was gone.'

Every person on the tour was mesmerised by Jules's story, including Richard, Melanie and Harry.

'What type of creature was it?' Asked Melanie.

'I'll come to that soon.'

'Sorry to interrupt you, Jules. Please continue.'

'The Zoo proprietor offered a large reward to anyone who could recapture the creature. This was added to by the police when the body of a sailor was found one night - well, what was left of him.' Everyone in the group gasped.

'I have a feeling this story is going to make me a bit squeamish.'

'Just my type of story, Melanie,' said Richard.

'Everyone assumed it was the creature that had attacked and eaten the sailor. Soon, another case was reported nearby, then another. In total ten people were attacked and killed in the vicinity of these warehouses. Eventually they were abandoned, and no ship would moor anywhere near them. Even to this day, fisherman coming back to the harbour late at night have reported seeing a strange creature swimming in the harbour waters. The creature, they say, has the body of a man and the head of a crocodile. So on that note, I think we'd better leave the warehouses. I'm sure I saw something moving in the water behind you...' Every one turned and looked behind, laughing nervously and holding onto their partners.

'Thank you for coming on the tour. I hope you enjoyed yourselves. Do tell all your friends to join the next tour.' The group clapped and thanked Jules before slowly dissipating towards the late night bars that were still open, except for Richard, Melanie and Harry who stared at the still water of the harbour in front of the warehouses.

'Wow! That *was* a scary story. The best of them all,' said Harry.

'It certainly was. I wonder how much of it is true?' Asked Melanie.

'None of it! It's just a story, like the rest. You must know these stories start off as total fiction and over the ages they become legends with a hint of possibility,' said Harry.

'I think that last story was all true, Melanie.' Richard was now teasing her.

'Ha ha, very funny.' Melanie felt a sudden chill and wrapped her arms around herself.

'In fact, look there! I'm sure I saw the water move. Maybe the creature is coming to get you!'

'I don't get sacred that easily.'

'Actually, something did move there,' said Harry.

'Don't you start now!'

'No, I'm serious! Look there. It looks big.' They stared at the surface of the harbour water where Harry was pointing, and saw that something had created large ripples in the water. They watched as the ripples disappeared and the light from the harbour buildings were again reflected on the surface.

'Over there!' Richard pointed further along the quayside to where the water had again been disturbed. He walked at a fast pace towards the disturbance.

'It's probably just a large fish or something. Why don't we just go and have a drink at one of those bars instead,' suggested Melanie.

'Come on, let's see where it's going,' said Harry, and ran to join Richard, who was already way ahead, approaching some warehouses that had not yet been renovated. Melanie followed them as they disappeared around the corner of one of the warehouses, where the harbour waters continued along a small side canal.

'Richard! Harry! Slow down. Wait for me!'

Harry reappeared from around the corner warehouse. 'Come on, Melanie, catch up. We don't want to lose sight of it. It went up the side canal here.' Richard waited until they both had caught up with him, and then all three proceeded at a fast pace along the canal, on either side of which were further dilapidated warehouses. They stopped when they saw a wet patch in front of the canal path they were on that led into an unlit tunnel ahead.

'I think something got out of the water here and went in there,' said Richard, pointing at the tunnel.

'You don't think it's the creature, do you?' asked Harry, not really sure himself if he was being serious.

'Come on guys, you're scaring me now,' said Melanie.

'It's probably just a beaver or something,' said Richard.

'There are no beavers in Marseille, as far as I know,' said Melanie.

'Maybe a big water rat then.'

They all jumped and took a step backwards when they heard a scratching noise coming from the tunnel.

'What was that noise?' said Harry.

'I'm not sure.'

'Come on, let's go,' said Melanie, feeling more and more agitated the longer they stayed there. She screamed when a cat came out of the tunnel and ran past them at lightning speed, followed by a large rat. Then more and more rats started coming out.

'Run!' shouted Richard, as he turned and fled as fast as his legs could carry him, followed closely behind by Melanie and Harry. They looked down at the ground as they ran and saw the rats scampering past them all running in the same direction. They turned the harbour corner into the open space where the tour guide had been talking earlier, and stopped to catch their breaths as they watched the rats scatter in all directions.

'It's just rats!' said Richard. He held his knees, winded by the sudden dash. In fact all three of them did the same thing.

'I must get back to the gym when we get home. That was pathetic!'

'It was a bit. If there was a real creature it would have got us by now,' said Melanie. They all burst into fits of laughter.

'Come on, let's get a drink. I'm in need of one now!' said Richard. They walked to the end of the harbour where several bars were still blaring out music, busy with late night drinkers and revellers

Unseen by the three English Students as they chatted and enjoyed drinking at the bars, a creature moved out of the darkness of the tunnel into the light of a flickering lamppost. Had they stayed, they would have seen not a water rat, but a creature with claw like feet, at the end of which were sharp talons, supporting a scaly human shaped body, on top of which was the head of a crocodile, with sharp teeth and yellow lizard eyes. It was chewing something that it held in its scaly clawed hands. The creature took one more bite, threw a leather boot into the water, and then disappeared back into the darkened tunnel.

Printed in Great Britain
by Amazon

58871173R00122